TO SOMEONE
Jimmy's story continues

PETER MEADOWS

A Countdown Books Paperback

First published in Great Britain in 2011 by Matador.

This edition published in 2011 by Countdown,
146 Bethnal Green Road, London E2 6DG.

2nd Edition.

ISBN 978 - 0 - 9570986 - 0 - 2
A CIP Catalogue Record for this book is available from the British Library.
Printed in the UK by Sterling Financial Print, ME8 0PZ.
Cover artwork by Paul McEvoy @ Bold Graphic Design.

PREFACE

As Jimmy sauntered away from the crashing waves, the cry of seagulls echoing his cry for help, the noise of crunching pebbles beneath his tired feet, and the vapour of the salty sea air harsh against his young skin, this has exasperated young Jimmy, nothing seems right anymore. He is left with a savoury taste in his mouth, a tangled mass of despair and yet elation, his mind awash with hatred, disappointment and anxiety... fuelled with and exaggerated by the gin and amphetamines, which only added to his fragile state of mind – where does he go from here?

Lost, disillusioned, frightened and alone, he had been through many sequences of travesty and betrayal, he has to carry on – after all, surely things could not get any worse? Jimmy is one of life's survivors, after all he was a mod, a cut above the rest, far more superior than his peers. He was no cop-out, he was not going to let those bastards get him down. As Jimmy heads off into the unknown, an extraordinary sequence of events unfold – acquaintances from a darker side of city life add to the complex yet colourful tapestry of his young life and, just when you think you know where it is heading, whack! Another unexpected twist greets you with a vengeance.

As Jimmy's wayward attitude encompasses him, we see another side emerge. A side that bears no resemblance to his former self, yet which has all the hallmarks of the character we have all grown to know and love. As the years roll by Jimmy finds himself surrounded by the clique that he had left behind... which is why things start hotting up, with violent twists and disturbing turns, and which seems to sum up this rollercoaster white knuckle ride. As Jimmy's life rages into the 90's, you'll discover that it's beyond your expectations. I mean, let's face it... To be someone is a wonderful thing.

Wolfy the Mod

Childhood dreams, hopes, expectations of what lies ahead on your journey of life. We were all there, we dreamt of being a somebody then you leave school and the reality is you're a nobody just like the bloke you passed every day on your way to school, the one that swept the road, the one you and your mates took the piss out of.

There's four kinds of people, the plodders like the road sweep, the jammy bastards that can do no wrong, you know, the sort that if they fell in a bucket of shit they'd come out smelling of roses, and then there's the unlucky fuckers like me that if I fell in a bucket of tits I'd come out sucking my thumb and at the top of the tree there's the somebodies. This is the story of my life so far and how I've spent most of it trying to be someone, the highs, the lows, the regrets and the laughs. When the day comes and I'm an old git sitting there in my incontinence pants stinking of piss looking back at my life would I have changed anything?

There comes a point in most people's lives where they stop and think what am I doing, where am I going, why did I do that, what is life all about and is it worth living. For most it comes later in life, maybe after a failed marriage or business or like me you just feel life's let you down, it ain't lived up to your expectations.

For me it came at eighteen, yep eighteen, still a poxy kid, how sad is that? It came as I sat on a rock in the pissing rain somewhere off the south coast. The rock looked so peaceful and beautiful from the shore so I nicked a boat and headed out towards it. I climbed onto the rock and let the boat drift off but now I'm sitting here soaking wet on the worst come down I've ever had; it's like a lot of things in life, it ain't what it seemed, it's just another thing that's let me down. It looked the perfect place to end it all, but now I'm sobering up from the bottle of Gilbey's gin I downed on the way out here, it didn't seem a very good idea. I threw the empty bottle of gin in the sea and watched it fill with water, it didn't take long for the bubbles to stop as it gently sunk to the sand below. I stood up ready to jump in and breathe the crystal clear water into my lungs and sink like the discarded empty bottle, but I just couldn't do it. It shit the life out of me, I mean it ain't instant is it, I should have just jumped in front of the train instead of getting on it and coming here. Now I'm stuck on this poxy rock and the way my luck's going I'll probably get hypothermia and end up getting eaten by these fucking crabs that are crawling round my feet.

I say the way my luck was going but looking back I suppose I brought it all on myself really. I fucked up big time, you see I got nicked at Brighton while having one of our many seaside battles with the Rockers. Now that was bad enough but when I got home I had an almighty row with my Mum and Dad, I ended up packing my stuff and leaving.

I spent two nights kipping under the Hammersmith Flyover. I got a job as a dustman, I lasted two days, fuck that carrying shit around for a poxy nine quid a week.

There was this bird I really fancied, Bunny her nickname was, my mate Dave said I should steer clear of her, he reckoned she was called Bunny coz she fucked like a rabbit and everyone had had her, nothing wrong with that I thought so I did as well on the beach! Anyway, when we get home there she is at the Goldhawk with Dave and she walked straight past me. The final straw was when I come off my GS in the pissing rain, that scooter was my pride and joy and there it was all smashed and twisted on the side of the road.

So here I am soaking wet sitting on this poxy rock waiting to turn blue and die but then in the distance I could see this fishing boat and it appeared to be heading towards me. I started shouting and waving my arms around like a lunatic, a bit like that nutty drummer out The Who, anyway it worked, he saw me and took me back to Brighton, back to the harbour where I nicked the boat some five hours earlier.

I walked down the sea front and headed towards the pier. When I got there I bought some fish and chips and a nice big mug of tea. I continued walking down the coast road not quite knowing where I was going or what I was doing when I saw something that made me stop in my tracks. On the other side of the road there he was, the Ace Face, the coolest Mod and what was he doing, he was only patching up the hotel that three days earlier he was so happy smashing up along with about fifty other Mods! I was fascinated, I just sat and watched in total disbelief, how could this be, I mean he was the epitome of cool. In the Aquarium Ballroom he was the one that everyone copied. He'd do a new dance and by the end of the night everyone was doing it, that's power for you!

The more and more I watched, the more I was getting wound up so I thought fuck it I'll go and confront him. By the time I'd crossed the busy road he was up a ladder cleaning the windows.

"Oi you, you up there."

"Me."

"Yeah you Mr odd job man."

"Who wants to know?"

"Me Jimmy, I wanna know, I wanna know why Mr Ace Face is a fucking odd job man."

He got down from that ladder pretty sharpish and he didn't look too happy.

"My name's Ray and what the fuck's it got to do with you what I do."

"Nothing, I suppose, I just had you down as something more than this."

"Well let me tell you Jimmy things ain't all that they seem, see that Jag over there."

"Yeah."

"Well its mine."

"Bollocks.

"Alright Jim I'll prove it, there's the key, open it up and in the glove box are two tickets for the ballroom Saturday night."

Well I got inside and he was right. I looked over and he was chatting to his boss then he went with him back into the hotel, I don't know what came over me but I started it up, whacked it in drive and I was off. I weren't too sure where I was off to but I knew I had to get away from Brighton, London and my whole life, I needed a clean start.

The Jag had a full tank of juice so I decided to head north and when the juice ran out that's where I'll settle. Now I don't know a lot about motors but I thought a full tank would get me a bit further than bleedin' Watford. No offence to the good people of Watford but I couldn't see myself settling there, for one reason, it's only about twenty mile from London. The main reason is my aunt Flo lives there and she was always banging on about how she fucking hated it and wished she'd stayed in London and I certainly didn't wanna settle anywhere near that old bag. I didn't have a clue where to go, the furthest north I'd ever been was bleedin' Enfield and that was only coz I fell a kip on the train and missed my stop, so I shut my eyes and stuck a pen in the map, Manchester was where I was heading.

The only thing I knew about Manchester was it's got a good football team and it was a fucking long train journey. I got to Manchester at about ten and found a cheap B & B by the station, it was a right shit-hole but the bed was comfortable enough. I only had enough money for a couple of nights so the plan was to get a good night's kip then start looking for work nice and early in the morning. As soon as my head hit the pillow I was out of it, so out of it I didn't wake up till about ten thirty, so much for an early start. The day just seemed to get worse, it didn't stop bleedin' raining, I was soaked.

Well, I don't know whether it was my accent or the fact I was starting to look a bit grubby, everyone I approached for work weren't interested. I was starting to get a bit worried, all I had was the clothes on my back, a couple of quid and the blues, no not the blues that some old black bloke sings about while strumming a fucking guitar, although I was pretty low, no these were the French blues I bought from Rudy the local dealer. If I was gonna make a new start then they had to go. I swear it was down to the drugs that made everyone think I was fucking nuts, I didn't know whether I was coming or going myself half the time. What I should have done was flush them down the khasi. They'd caused me nothing but grief so far but if I could flog them then it gave me another couple of days up here. Now blues ain't the sort of thing you can just flog on the corner of the street so I had to make myself presentable, so I could get into one of the clubs. I managed to nick a shirt and pair of trousers, I didn't look as sharp as I normally did but I weren't on the pull so it didn't matter.

Well there certainly weren't no shortage of clubs to choose from, the city centre was buzzing. I ended up in a club called Sally's, bit of a strange name for a club, I suppose a bird called Sally owned it. Anyway the place was heaving, there was crumpet everywhere it was fucking amazing. I've gone to the bar and got myself a pint but before it's touched my lips the bird next to me said, "Hey, you're from London right?"

"Yes love"

"So what brings you north then?"

"I'm Jimmy by the way what's your name?"

"Cindy."

"Well Cindy I'm up 'ere on a bit of business."

"And what business is that Jimmy boy?"

"Er, less of the boy thank you very much, as it 'appens you might be able to help me out there, are you and yer mates alright for pills?"

"Why what yer got?"

"Blues."

"Wait there I'll be back in a minute."

Cindy's minute turned into five then ten, by fifteen I decided to have a wander. I've gone to the bog, when I've come out there she is stood there with two of the biggest geezers I've ever seen, one of them has grabbed my arm and said,

"So Jimmy, you've got some Blues 'ave yer."

At first I thought they were a couple of local dealers and they're gonna relieve me of my little stash but no my shit day was about to get a whole lot worse.

"Yeah I got a few."

No sooner had I spluttered out my last nervous word, I suddenly became airborne; the other geezer's grabbed my other arm and I swear my feet didn't touch the ground. It was all highly embarrassing and undignified as I was dragged across the packed club and into a room behind the bar. I felt like a right prat. I'd only gone and picked the one club that had a serious drug problem and unless they curbed it, it was gonna be shut down. So it was bad enough I was gonna lose the blues and be left with fuck all but what started out to be a bad day that got worse had now turned into the worst fucking nightmare imaginable, they only went and called the Old Bill! If I'd known the fifteen minutes it took for the Old Bill to get there was gonna be my last fifteen minutes of freedom for eight years, I would have took my chances with the smaller bouncer and made a dash for it. I was arrested and taken down the station where I was charged for drug dealing.

I was banged up in a cell and due in court first thing Monday morning. Now I thought the B & B I was staying in was a shit-hole but compared to the cell I was now residing in, it was the fucking Ritz! It was about ten foot square, cold and it stunk of piss; once I'd read the graffiti scratched on the walls I just sat there, head in my hands in total despair. Where did it all go wrong, how did I go from a very cocky but happy and sometimes confused teenage to a near suicidal, scooter wrecking, car taking, drug dealing and in my Mum's words little animal? Well sitting here in my piss stenched cell, I had all the time in the world to try and work it out, well two days in fact before I was due in court.

To work out where it all went wrong, I suppose I'd have to go back to when I was a kid, I was probably no different to any other kid, I dreamt of being a racing car driver or pop star or in the movies. I was gonna be a somebody and not a nobody like my Dad. He was alright, I don't suppose he was any different from all the other kids' dads. I used to watch him sitting there in front of the tele with a dirty string vest stretched over his fat gut, bottle of beer in one hand, fag in the other, burping and farting all night till he finally past out coz he was so pissed. Nah I wanted more outta life than that, I wanted the fucking world.

I never stopped wanting to be that somebody and that's why I was a Mod. It felt good to belong to a new generation of fashion conscious teenagers that didn't give a shit, it was an escape from normality. I had respect from my mates, when we were out we could of took on the fucking world. I wanted to live life to the full, so much so that somewhere along the way I got lost, lost in a world of pure self indulgence. I didn't give a shit about anything or anybody, life was one big laugh, the drugs, the booze, the clothes the good times were mine but then that weekend in Brighton changed everything.

In the space of three days I'd fallen in love, yep love the most powerful emotion, it felt great, only trouble was she didn't love me. It was just a bit of fun, a quick bunk up on the beach so then I had to deal with rejection. I felt let down by everything, the last straw that well and truly broke the camel's back was seeing the Ace face working as a fucking odd job man. I just wanted to end it all, I felt let down, I didn't, and here I am in a poxy cell wishing I did.

What was to be the longest two days of my life came to an end; there I stood in court charged with drug dealing and to my surprise vehicle theft. It turns out that my Mum was actually worried about me and reported me as a missing person, last seen boarding a train to Brighton. The Old Bill put two and two together and it didn't take long for them to link the Jag to me as well. It was comforting to know that after all I'd done, my Mum was still concerned about me. I mean Manchester is a fucking long way to come for someone who doesn't like travel. That concern was short lived: when she stood there in court and the charges were read out, she turned round and walked straight out. I think she thought I was getting done for just having drugs not selling them.

My day in court didn't go well, the judge weren't too impressed I'd been in court a week earlier for rioting in Brighton. I was expecting to go down but when he said four years I nearly shit myself, four fucking years, now I've just spent two days in a cell and that seemed like a fucking lifetime, now I really did wish I'd jumped in front of that train! They let Mum have a quick word with me before they took me to prison and it didn't matter how much I explained to her I weren't a drug dealer she didn't believe me and she shot off home on the first train she could.

I'd heard a lot about prison and I can tell you I was more than a little bit worried, I ain't the biggest of geezers and they were sending me to Strangeways which ain't a borstal for naughty kids, it's a proper fucking prison. It was only about a ten minute ride to the prison, the prison guard I was handcuffed to was alright. He told me prison was a bit like school or when you start work, he said there's a pecking order. Well, when I walked through that prison I didn't so much feel like small fry in an ocean of big fish, I was so far down the food chain I was more like fucking plankton.

The guard told me, just keep your head down, mind your own business, do your time and you'll get out in one piece. Well, looking round at all the Neanderthals milling round, that's exactly what I intended to do. The prison guard was spot on when he said it was a bit like school. You had the bully, now the bully didn't tend to be the toughest kid, he was somewhere in the middle, not quite in with the main gang but above the weakest kids, you know the kids that were always the last choice when we were picking the football teams. Anyway I'd been in for a week now and I'd sussed out who the prison number one was and now it was time to meet the bully. He was a big fat Geordie geezer with ginger hair, a real ugly fucker, his name was Henry. I was quite relieved he was the bully, coz he'd been eyeing me up all week. If he'd been the prison poof I wouldn't of stood a chance in the showers! It was dinner time when he decided to introduce himself.

"Do you mind if I sit next to you Jimmy."

"No be my guest."

"My name's Henry, so Jimmy you're a cockney bastard."

"No mate I'm not a cockney and I do 'appen to have both parents."

"You're from London right."

"Yeah I'm from London."

"Exactly, so that makes you a cockney bastard."

Before I've got time to explain that I was from Shepherd's Bush and not East London, he's only gone and grabbed the two sausages off my plate and said,

"You don't mind do yer, only I'm fucking starving!"

Now I weren't too upset about losing the two sausages that were slipping round my plate in a pool of cheap grease but Henry was well and truly taking the piss and unless I made a stand now and taught this ugly fucker to give me a bit of respect my four years in here were gonna be hell so I said,

"No mate I tell yer what, 'ave the fucking lot."

I got the plate in the palm of my hand and smashed it in his fat face. I hit him with everything I had, he went flying backwards and ended up on the deck, and before he could regain his composure and react there were two guards on me and two pulling him to his feet. The sight of baked beans, mashed potato and blood from his busted nose trickling down his face, had the entire dining hall pissing themselves laughing. It reminded me a bit of Laurel and Hardy, you know all that custard pie in the face stuff. Anyway, as funny as it was it cost me a week in solitary.

I sat there all week not knowing whether or not I'd done the right thing, my Dad always brought me up not to take shit from anyone. He always said get the first punch in and coz I weren't the biggest kid, he always said the bigger they are the harder they fall, which was true but the bigger they are the harder they hit back and Henry was a big fucker alright. Ain't it funny, when you want time to go quick it drags on and when you want it to drag on it flies by. Well my week flew by and there I am queuing up to get my breakfast. I was shitting myself, I picked my tray up, turned round and there he was two tables in front of me. He still had the plaster across his nose holding it straight. I had to walk past him to get to the back of the hall; as I got closer I was expecting the evil eye and the intimidating snarl but instead he just put his head down and carried on stuffing his fat face with corn flakes. As I passed him I can't tell yer how relieved I was but then all of a sudden my heart stopped, someone grabbed my arm from behind. I was expecting to be spun round and decked but instead there was a skinny geezer standing there. "Jim over here mate there's someone who'd like to meet you." As we worked our way through the tables I suddenly realised we were heading towards the boss's table, the prison number one. As I approached the table he pointed to an empty chair. "Sit down son," what a relief, a Londoner, "let me introduce myself, I'm Mr Warren and that's Ian, Rob over there and the ugly git on the end that's Steve."

"Nice to meet yer, what a relief I was beginning to think I was the only Londoner up here."

"You're amongst friends here Jim, so what brings you north then, what you been up to?"

"I got caught selling drugs in one of the clubs didn't I?"

"You've got a lot of guts Jim, what you done to Henry last week was fucking priceless, I ain't laughed so much since I got here."

"I'm glad you enjoyed the show."

"Can't say I like the fact you're a dealer though, I ain't got a lot of time for drugs but still it took balls trying to sell 'em up here."

"That's the thing, I ain't a fucking dealer I was just trying to sell my personal stash so I could stay up here a bit longer."

"Now I know you're bullshitting me, who the fuck in their right mind would want to stay in a shit-hole like Manchester?"

"It's a long story, but perhaps you're right, I ain't in my right mind."

"Anyway, Jim I don't give a shit what you done, in here we're all equal, me and the lads like yer Jim and from now on you'll be alright welcome on board son."

I couldn't believe it, in the space of a couple of weeks I'd gone from the kid that no one wanted in the team to the top of the tree. The weeks soon turned into months and it didn't take long to get over the shock of having to face the next four years in here; being part of Mr Warren's crew made life a lot easier, I certainly never got any more hassle from Henry. Mr Warren was alright, he was a big bloke about forty, he was a laugh and considered himself just one of the lads. Like he said we're all equal in here but there was a dark side to him, I see him lose his rag one day, he didn't rant and rave or even raise his voice but he had this menacing look about him the sort of look that says don't fuck with me. It turns out that Mr Warren along with his brother run one of the most notorious London firms, he's now doing a six year stretch for money laundering and screwing the taxman.

In prison I felt important, I felt like I was part of something special, it felt a bit like when I was a Mod, I belonged to something. I was a somebody, deep down I knew I was just an eighteen year old kid with a lot of attitude and not a lot to back it up, who was having the worst run of bad luck fucking imaginable but somehow it felt right. I know that might sound fucking stupid but it felt like I was on a journey and this was the beginning of something special, call it a gut instinct but somehow I just knew it would all come right in the end.

The one thing there's no shortage of in prison is time; during the day it weren't so bad but at night when that cell door slammed shut and your lying in that dark cold cell your memory becomes your best friend. You dig deep into the recesses of your brain. Friday night was the worst night, I'd lie there running through what I'd be doing if I weren't banged up. I pictured myself picking my new suit up at five thirty, by six thirty I would have had my dinner, by seven thirty I would've had a soak in the bath and got ready, just in time to catch Ready Steady Go on the tele. By eight fifteen a blast on Dave's horn outside signalled the start of another night of non stop pill popping mayhem. It was fun, it was what being young and stupid was all about and ultimately what led to me now dreaming it instead of living it.

My only contact from outside was with Judy, poor Judy she had the misfortune of falling in love with me. Don't get me wrong, I like her and occasionally we'd have a bit of fun together but I didn't fancy her like she did me, I always had my sights set a bit higher. She used to write to me, tell me all the gossip, I always looked forward to her letters, she was the only one who believed me. She saw the mixed up stupid Jimmy who was in the wrong place at the wrong time unlike the others who thought I was a fucking nut case. As the months turned to years, the letters eased off, she eventually met a Yank and fucked off to live in America. She still wrote occasionally but I wanted to know what Dave, Ron, Charlie and the others were up to, I didn't want to know how wonderful the Grand Canyon was or Niagara fucking Falls, I didn't give a shit about her little adventures in the States.

Time soon went and before I knew it I'd done three years, I'd somehow managed to avoid getting caught for my involvement of Mr. Warren's various dodgy scams and I was hoping for early release. I owed Mr Warren a lot, my three years in here were a breeze compared to most. There were blokes in here that hated me, that given the chance would have beat the shit out of me a long time ago if it hadn't been for the protection I got from him, blokes like Henry. His nickname was Henry Chopper Wilson, the reason for his colourful nickname was when he was out hard at work on a nightshift servicing machines, his mate was busy servicing his darling wife. When he found out he walks into his mate's local, calmly buys him a pint and as he put his hand on the bar Henry pulls out a hatchet and chops three of the geezer's fingers off. Now most people would be pretty pissed off losing three fingers but when you're tipped to be the next national tennis champion it must be pretty fucking devastating. Yep the geezer I decided to share my dinner with in that first week was Henry Chopper Wilson, the prison psycho!

As you can imagine Henry hated me but there was one bloke he hated more and that was Mr Warren, partly because of the protection he gave me but mainly because Mr Warren made Henry's life hell in here. You see Mr Warren was a big tennis fan and he didn't take too kindly to Henry chopping off one of the top player's fingers. Henry was one scary bloke, even though I had the protection from Mr Warren and the lads, I did my best to avoid him. Mr Warren on the other hand never missed a chance to take the piss out of him and have a laugh at his expense. Well you can only take the piss for so long, everyone's got a breaking point and Mr Warren was about to find Henry's. It was a Thursday afternoon as we were heading back to the cells, it'd been a pretty uneventful day, not a lot happens day to day inside but for Henry it was probably the worst day of his life, he'd got news that morning that his Mum died. I weren't that close to my Mum so I like most of the others didn't see it as a big deal but Henry, well he was devastated as he was pretty close to his Mum.

He'd been acting weird all day, he just looked vacant, all the lights were on but there was no one in, if you know what I mean. I was on the landing having a chat with Mr Warren when out of the corner of my eye I could see Henry coming towards us. Now just the sight of Henry made me nervous, I couldn't believe that someone as hard and nutty like him could take the sort of shit that Mr Warren dished out on a day to day basis. So I just kept my guard up when he was around, unlike Mr Warren, he didn't give a shit. I don't think Mr Warren even noticed him as he got closer, but I did, I could see his eyes fixed on Mr Warren. If Raquel Welch walked past with her tits out, I don't think Henry would have noticed, he was on a mission.

My heart rate must have doubled, the adrenalin was pumping round my body but Mr Warren just kept on laughing and joking, then in a split second a screwdriver dropped from Henry's sleeve but before I could say anything he's gone and stuck it straight in Mr Warren's side, he hit the deck instantly. Henry's pulled it out but before he's got a chance to finish him off, I grabbed him from behind, pulled him back, we've both gone over, I fell on the landing. Henry's gone flying down the metal stairs, it seemed to take ages for him to land at the bottom. I got up and was ready for him but he just lay there in a crumpled heap on the floor.

Within seconds there were guards everywhere, Mr Warren was rushed to hospital and I was banged up in my cell like everyone else. It must have been an hour later before they came to get me for questioning; they led me passed the staircase where Henry was still lying at the bottom. He'd only gone and broke his fucking neck, he was as dead as a Dodo. I was interviewed by a couple of detectives and charged with manslaughter, they didn't believe a word I said, there were no witnesses to back my story up. No one saw the psychotic look in Henry's eyes, no one felt the fear or the adrenalin pumping round their body, all they heard was Henry flying down the stairs and all they saw was me standing at the top. The Old Bill had their own version of what happened, the way they see it was that me and Henry had a bit of history. Mr Warren like usual was having a go at him, a fight broke out and I pushed Henry down the stairs, and that's exactly how the judge saw it. Mr Warren ended up with a punctured lung and a little scar and I ended up with another five years at Her Majesty's Pleasure. To say I was gutted was an understatement, I was fucking devastated. Can you imagine, there's me looking forward to early release then I go and end up getting another five years, five fucking years, that's what I'd already done plus another two on top of that. I'll be twenty fucking six by the time I get out. It was bad enough I was getting banged up for another five years but I had to serve it in a different nick so it was like starting all over again, at least I had the protection from Mr Warren and the lads at Strangeways. On the upside I was being sent to the Scrubs in London which is only ten minutes from my house. I know I couldn't pop home for a cup of tea or anything but it felt good knowing I was heading back to my neighbourhood.

The initial fear I had when I was first sent down wasn't there, instead it was more a nervous apprehension, it was the not knowing what to expect. In Strangeways, I had respect, I'd done the prison psycho and I was part of Mr Warren's crew. After a couple of days I settled in and soon discovered my reputation preceded me, lucky for me two of Mr Warren's firm were currently residing in the Scrubs. One was a huge hard looking bloke called Eddy and the other was a normal looking bloke called Nick. There was no Mr Warrens in the Scrubs, no prison hierarchy, everyone seemed to keep themselves to themselves and get on with their time, I suppose Eddy probably got more respect than most partly coz he was a right hard bastard but mainly coz of his connections on the outside. I clicked with Eddy straight away, he was a good laugh, but it was only ever gonna be a short lived friendship, he was due out in six months but it was long enough for the rest of the prison population to see that I was well connected and hopefully when Eddy was released my time inside would be trouble free. The six months flew by and while Eddy was gathering up his few belongings I stopped by for a last chat.

"Jimmy cheer up mate."

"Cheer up, it's easy for you to say you're getting outta 'ere."

"Jim I ain't said this before mate but I don't think you realise just how lucky you are."

"Lucky, you 'aving a laugh or what, how the fuck do you work that one out."

"Jim from what you tell me you've been caught up in a whole heap of shit, but listen to me son one thing I've learnt is things 'appen for a reason. You can be in the right place at the right time or the wrong place at the wrong time. You might not think it now Jim but when you saved Mr Warren's arse you was most definitely in the right place, so what you got Jim, three, four years?"

"No, five, five fucking years, that makes me twenty six when I get out."

"Twenty six, that's no fucking age, trust me you'll want for nothing when you get out of 'ere."

"Now Jim I don't wanna rub salt in the wound or anything but when I've recovered from being on the piss for a couple of days is there anything I can do for yer."

"Yeah, there is as it goes, I ain't seen or heard from my family since I've been in here, I don't suppose you can pop round and 'ave a chat with 'em, now I'm only a few stops away on the bus they might wanna see me."

"No problem Jim stick the address down on there then fuck off, you're depressing me, and Jim remember, keep your head down, do your time and you'll be alright, trust me."

And that was that, I fucked off back to my cell and Eddy fucked off outta 'ere leaving me with plenty to think about.

All the time I was up north I never asked or questioned about Mr Warren, to be honest I didn't really give a shit who or what he was. All I knew was it was better to have him as a friend than an enemy but now I'm serving another five years as a result of that friendship, I decided to do a bit of digging and Nick was the perfect bloke to fill me in. "Nick you got a minute?"

"A minute, I've got thirty fucking years, sit down Jim what can I do for yer."

"Mr Warren, who the fuck is he?"

"You know who he is."

"All I know is he's some sort of big shot gangster."

"He was Jim, now he leaves all that gangster shit to his brother Mike, Mr Warren's more of a big shot businessman these days."

"And what sort of business is that then."

"Property Jim, he owns most of the pubs and clubs in London and also a chain of bookies."

"He's worth a few bob then."

"He's fucking minted Jim, worth millions he is."

"If he's just a businessman how's he end up getting a six year stretch?"

"Well let's just say his bank manager didn't exactly give him a business loan to start that little empire up. The Old Bill's been after him for years and if it weren't for his brother they still would be."

"Why, what's his brother do."

"It's a long story Jim."

"That's alright we've got plenty of time."

"You don't need to know, but I'll tell yer this, now you listen and you listen good, when you get outta here Mr Warren will see you alright, he's a fair bloke and he rewards loyalty. When he does Jim you take your money and get out of this shit, do yer hear what I'm saying?"

"Yeah loud and clear."

That night I couldn't sleep, my head was buzzing with a million thoughts. How generous would I be if someone saved my life, but not only saved it they then went on to do five years as a result of it. If it was me I'd be very grateful, I'd make sure they were set up for life.

Six months had passed since Eddy was released and I was still on a high, it felt like I'd won the pools. I know I couldn't do a lot coz I was still banged up but it gave me hope, a dream, something to look forward to, it kept me going, all of a sudden life in here didn't seem so bad. There was light at the end of the tunnel, alright that light was a long way off but it was there. Well, Eddy kept his promise, he had a word with my Mum, she wrote to me asking if I wanted her to visit. I weren't that close to my Mum, it was alright when I was a nipper but as I got older and started going out more she distanced herself from me a bit. I swear there were times she didn't even like me, I think she had a problem with most blokes. My Dad was a right fucking slob and she seemed to judge all blokes by him, my sister on the other hand couldn't do no wrong, the sun well and truly shone out of her arse; anyway I wrote back and said course I didn't. Well, the day of reckoning came, I've walked into the visitors' hall and there she was sitting there with her hair rollers in; it'd been nearly four years since I last saw her, she didn't look any different.

"Hello Mum, how you doing."

"I'm fine Jim, you look alright, you've put a bit of weight on, it suits yer."

"I didn't expect to see yer."

"At the end of the day you're still my son."

"Is that right coz the last time I was at home you couldn't wait to see the back of me, you loved it when I packed and left, good riddance you said."

"What, you don't think I regret what I said, of course I do, but at the time me and yer Dad weren't getting on too well, I had a lot to deal with, I was stressed out."

"What do yer mean at the time, you never got on, you're always fucking rowing?"

"Jim less of that language, I'm still your mother, and as it 'appens me and your Dad used to be very 'appy."

"When was that then coz I never saw it."

"Before you and your sister came along."

"Thanks very much, I love you too."

"Jim whatever you and your sister get up to, me and your Dad never stopped loving yer. I'm not blaming you two it was us, we just stopped trying, instead of a couple we became a family. We devoted all our time on you kids, then when you grew up all of a sudden, we didn't 'ave anything in common anymore. If it weren't for you kids, we probably would of split up years ago."

"So if you were that unhappy why are you still with him?"

"Because since you've been locked up things 'ave changed, we get on a lot better, and before you say anything it's not because we were glad to see the back of yer it's because well, Jim, you're an uncle."

"Fuck mine, you mean my perfect, can't do no fucking wrong sister ain't the little angel you thought she was, when did she 'ave it?"

"Four months after you was locked up, that's another reason I was glad to see the back of yer, she chose the same weekend to tell me she was expecting as you decided to run riot in bleedin' Brighton."

"All I done was have a bit of fun at the seaside."

"It was too much Jim, I couldn't deal with you, her and your useless Dad, I would've ended up in a bleedin' nut house."

"So it was easier to say goodbye Jim and good riddance and deal with Sarah."

"You were out of control Jim, when you got sent down there was nothing I could do to help yer so I put all my energy into Sarah and the baby."

"What's she 'ave then."

"A boy, his name's Steven."

"You got any photos of him?"

"I'll bring some next time, he's a lovely lad, your Dad idolises him, it's been a blessing in disguise really, me and yer Dad are a lot happier now, I just wish you could be part of it."

"Well that ain't gonna 'appen for a while yet."

"Jim you're such a prat, why did yer do it, you'd be out of here by now if you'd just……"

"Just what, just step back and watch a mate get killed. A mate I might add that if it weren't for him it might have been me with a screwdriver in me. Mr Warren was fucking good to me."

"If you say so, I still think you were bleedin' stupid."

"No one wishes more than me I weren't there but I was and shit 'appens, anyway who's the kid's dad?"

"I haven't got a clue, she wouldn't tell us, you know what your Dad's like, he would of killed him if he found out, she said it was just some lad she met at a party but I don't believe that for a minute."

"Why's it so hard to believe, she was no different from any other teenage girl and I was no different either, all we wanted was a laugh, a bit of fun. The trouble with your generation is coz you had a shit time as teenagers because of the war you resented us having a good time, you was plain fucking jealous.".

"Rubbish."

"No it's not and I don't blame yer, who's to say that if half the" male teenage population weren't getting their bollocks shot off by the fucking Germans, you and yer mates would have been playing with 'em and you might of ended up like Sarah as well."

"Jim what's 'appened to yer, you'd never talk to me like that."

"What's 'appened to me, take a look around in case you hadn't noticed, this is a prison, not a fucking holiday camp, I've spent the last four years with murderers, gangsters and all sorts of fucking weirdos."

"Is it that bad love?"

"It can be if your face don't fit, I've been lucky I'm in with the right crowd."

"Good."

"So why after four years 'ave you decided you've got a son again?"

"I suppose 'aving Sarah's boy around all the time it brings back happy memories of when you was a kid and after talking to your mate Eddy it made us realise that perhaps you weren't such a bad lad after all. I can't change the past Jim, I've done the whole guilt trip, if only I hadn't let you leave, none of this would've 'appened routine, you can't keep going over the past so let's look to the future."

"That's easy for you to say, you ain't gotta spend the next four years in this shit-hole."

"No Jim I ain't but you're still a young man, you'll be twenty."

"Twenty fucking six, when I get out."

"Leave it out Jim, twenty six is no age, that's how old I was when I had you."

"Exactly, that's what scares the shit out of me."

"Why?"

"What do yer mean why, you've just sat there and told me you and Dad were happy as a couple of pigs in shit, till me and Sarah came along."

"That's right we were, I'm not saying as soon as you get out you've gotta rush out and start a bleedin' family, I'm just saying you're still a young man when you get out of 'ere."

"Yeah, I suppose you're right, I'll have a lot of living to do. I've missed out on a lot, I haven't heard from Dave and the others since I've been in 'ere, what they been up to, 'ave you heard anything?"

"The last I heard was Ron and Charlie were in the building game and Dave married that girl from The Three Horseshoes, you know the barmaid."

"What Bunny?"

"Yeah, I think that was her name, she was a right one she was, Sarah reckoned she was putting it about with everyone."

"Well that's fucking rich coming from her, she's not exactly sweet and innocent herself."

"That was her first time and she was unlucky."

"Whatever, she still can't do no fucking wrong can she."

"Well, compared to you, no she can't."

"So much for forgetting the past."

"Jim you was a little fucker and you know it so don't make out like you was the poor neglected little victim in all this."

"Calm down, language Mum."

"That's from being round you too long."

"You've only been 'ere ten minutes."

"Yeah, and all I've heard is fucking this, fucking that, it's bleedin' contagious.

"Look Jim I didn't come 'ere after four years to row."

"I know I'm sorry, let's start again, so where's Sarah and the kid staying."

"At home with me and your Dad, we put Steven in your old room."

"What did you do with all my gear?"

"It's in the loft."

"You should of just binned it, it ain't gonna be any good to me by the time I get out."

"Yeah you 'ave put on a few pounds ain't yer, at least they feed yer well."

"No they don't as it 'appens, the food in 'ere's crap, it's just that I got a cushy job in the kitchen, and what I meant was, it'll be no good to me when I get out coz it'll be out of fashion, I didn't mean it'll be no good coz I'm a fat bastard."

"I didn't say you were fat, in fact you look a lot better with a bit of meat on yer bones, you was always too skinny, trouble was you never gave yourself a chance to 'ave a decent meal, you was always flying off somewhere."

"So how's the old man, still pissed all the time is he?"

"He wasn't pissed all the time, he worked bloody hard and when he got in he liked to unwind with a few beers, what's wrong with that?"

"Nothing at all, we are all entitled to relax how we wanted, he chose to stay in and get pissed in front of the tele and I chose to go out and 'ave a laugh with my mates, but that was all wrong wasn't it?"

"Christ knows what you're gonna do when you get out of 'ere."

"I ain't got a clue but as that's not gonna 'appen for a while I ain't too worried, so come on is that it, surely after four years you've got a bit more news than that."

"Your cousin Terry got married."

"Jesus who'd marry that fucking idiot?"

"Remember that little blonde girl that always liked you."

"What Judy?"

"Yeah that's the one, well it was her mate Samantha."

"You're joking, she's fucking horrible."

"She's a lovely girl."

"She might 'ave a lovely personality but I've seen better looking things in the reptile house at London Zoo."

"Don't be so bleedin' nasty. I haven't seen that Judy for ages, she used to work on her Dad's stall at the market."

"She met some Yank and fucked off to America to live."

"How do you know?"

"Coz when I was sent down she was the only one who believed me and she always writes to me."

"It's a shame you never went out with her, you might not be where you are now if you had something else in your life other than riding round on bleedin' scooters all night getting up to no good with your mates."

"You're doing it again."

"What?"

"The past, I thought we was gonna forget about that and look to the future. Look Mum it's been great seeing yer again, I really appreciate it, we ain't got long left, are you gonna come again?"

"Yeah, course I will and next time there'll be no dragging up the past I promise yer, what's that bell?"

"That's time up."

"You don't get long do yer."

"It's long enough, I'll see yer next week hopefully."

"Yeah I'll do my best, take care Jim."

And that was that, I went back to my cell and Mum went back to the daily grind which is life.

Seeing Mum was a real tonic, I think I spoke more to her on that visit than I had in the whole year before I was sent down. Well considering I'd been banged up for nearly four years, judging by that conversation, I ain't missed out on a lot. I certainly ain't missed 'aving a screaming kid in the house, that would've done my fucking head in, and then there's my cousin Terry. Would I swap places with him, not in a million years, apart from the fact he's a fucking idiot, he ends up marrying a right horror and before you know it they'll 'ave a couple of snotty nose kids. They'll struggle to pay the bills and they'll end up saving all year for a poxy two week holiday in Selsy Bill or Bracklesham Bay and who am I to say it's wrong. I'm currently half way through an eight year prison term. No it's not wrong, if they're 'appy fair play to 'em, horses for courses and all that old bollocks but it's not my cup of tea, I want more out of life than that. Mum was true to her word, she was good as gold, every Thursday she'd turn up. To be honest the conversation bored me to tears but far better to 'ave a boring conversation about family than to 'ave my mates turn up and give me a blow by blow account of their Friday night, the Friday nights I missed so much.

Not too much exciting 'appens in prison, I done what I was told, minded my own business and before I knew it I'd already done another three years. Time in the Scrubs seemed to go even quicker, I think it helped seeing my Mum every week; there were a couple of occasions after she'd gone I actually thought being inside weren't so bad. She was a bit of a doom and gloom merchant my Mum. Well, things were going well like I say, then on Tuesday I was told I had a visitor; I knew it weren't my Mum coz she only came on a Thursday, I was hoping it'd be Dave or one of my other mates. Anyway, I've walked into the visitors' hall and there sitting in the corner was a very smart Mr Warren.

"'Ello Jim, how you doing son?"

We shook hands and he nearly broke my fucking fingers, he was genuinely pleased to see me.

"I'm not too bad as it goes."

"I'd like to give yer a big hug for what you did for me but I don't wanna risk creasing the suit!"

"Yeah that's a quality bit of cloth you got there."

"Saville Row's finest Jim, you're looking good, I'll 'ave to get you moved out them kitchens Jim before you put any more weight on! We don't want yer turning into a fat bastard do we now!"

"Yeah, you've got a point, my Mum thinks the same only she weren't so fucking harsh."

"So what's it like in 'ere, a lot better than up north I hope?"

"Yeah a lot better, so that cushy little number in the kitchen was down to you then?"

"Yeah."

"How did yer manage that then?"

26

"Let's just say the governor of this place is a friend of a friend.

"Cheers Mr Warren, I really appreciate that."

"Jim it's a job in a poxy kitchen, you sound so fucking grateful, I'm the grateful one 'ere, you saved my fucking life. Not only that but you've lost five of yours for the pleasure of it. By the way, when it's just you and me, drop the Mr Warren, it's Jack, anyone who done what you did is on first name basis, OK?"

"Yeah."

"Do you regret 'elping me out Jim?"

"I'll be totally honest with you Jack, if I could wind the clock back I would have watched Henry put more holes in yer than a fucking tea strainer. Not a day goes by that I don't regret being on that landing and what makes me laugh, when I got sent down 'ere, your mate Eddy reckons I was in the right place at the right time."

"My mate Eddy, no Jim he's not my mate he's my employee, I don't 'ave mates, and as for him saying you were in the right place at the right time, only time will tell. You're still a kid and you've got another two years in 'ere, so the way you see it, you were definitely in the wrong place. It's not until you're a lot older and you look back at your life will you know the true answer to that one, but for me Jim fortunately you were and I thank you for that. Have you thought about what you're gonna do when you get out?"

"I ain't really got a lot of options 'ave I?"

"No Jim you ain't, but lets face it you weren't exactly on the road to riches working as a fucking binman was yer?"

"No and that's why I told the boss."

"Yeah I know, to shove the job right up his arse."

"How the fuck did you know that?"

"Jim, I am where I am because I make it my business to know everything about everyone who has either the good fortune or misfortune of crossing my path. Jim I'm not one for small talk mate, I'm a busy man I've gotta be up the West End in thirty minutes, so I'm gonna shoot off but I'll leave yer with something to think about for the next two years. I've had a word with your Mum and she's given me your bank details and I've deposited fifteen grand."

"Fifteen grand, nice one, cheers."

"Jim shut the fuck up and let me finish. I'll be depositing fifteen grand for every year you've served for me, so seventy-five grand in total. What you do with it is up to you, you can buy a house or a little business, you can set yourself up for life with that or you can blow it all on flash cars and birds or snort half a ton of coke up your hooter for all I care, that's up to you Jim, but my debt to you is clear and our paths won't cross again. Did you get that Jim, Jim I said did you get that?"

"Yeah, yeah I did, sorry Jack I'm in shock mate, that's a fucking lot of money, thanks."

"Yeah it is and you deserve every penny, right I've said what I gotta say, I'm getting out of 'ere, look after yourself Jim and ease off the grub, the birds ain't gonna fancy yer if you're a fat fucker."

"Yeah I will, cheers Jack."

That night I couldn't sleep, I always knew Mr Warren would see me alright but seventy-five grand, that's a fucking lot of money. One thing for sure, I weren't too worried what I was gonna do when I got out, with that kind of money I could just 'ave a life of leisure!

Once the shock and excitement of knowing I was gonna be a rich bastard when I got out had worn off, I actually started to feel a bit pissed off, even depressed. You see I had this idea in my head that when I get out, I was gonna be part of Mr Warren's firm. I thought I'd run one of his clubs or other businesses, the truth is it felt good being one of the lads. I felt like I was a somebody but that ten minute chat with Mr Warren shattered all that. He went from being one of the lads to, I guess what he was, the boss. He made me feel like I was back at school or back at that fucking bin man job, I just felt insignificant and small.

All that we're on first name basis call me Jack was bollocks, he'd done his homework on me or should I say he got one of his employees as he called 'em to do it for him and he had my card well and truly marked! He was only confirming to me what I knew all along, that I was a fake, a pretender, I weren't no gangster. I was Jimmy the ex bin man that was in the wrong place at the wrong time. I didn't really fit in with the Mr Warrens and the Eddys of this world. Apart from shattering my hopes of being a big 'I am' when I get out, the worst thing about that ten minute conversation and my new found wealth was time just dragged on. It's a bit like when you're a kid you can't wait to grow up, you know life as an adult is great but you just seem stuck as a kid, boy did those school days drag on. Thursday came around quick enough though and Mum was there as usual. I think she was more excited about the money than me, she had it all planned out for me: I was gonna get out, buy a house, meet a nice girl, get married and live happy ever after; she seemed so happy I didn't have the heart to tell her that was the last thing I intended to do.

The next six months dragged on, it seemed to take longer to pass than the last two years, and it was fucking horrible knowing I had all that money but I still had another eighteen months before I could enjoy it. I became a bit ratty and frustrated and Mum didn't help by constantly banging on about what I should and shouldn't do with it. So when my Mum told me my Dad was coming to see me the following week, I was gonna let him have it big time. The last time I saw him, he was slumped in the armchair half cut, he couldn't be bothered to get up to wish me luck or anything, he didn't give a shit, he was just glad I was out of his life. When I walked into the visitors' hall and I saw him sitting there, it threw me out a bit. He looked so different: he'd had a shave, lost weight and his hair even looked washed and clean, instead of looking like he'd put his head in a fucking chip pan. He had a pathetic spanked puppy look about him, so I thought I'd give him a chance.

"Hello son."

"What you doing 'ere?"

"What do yer mean what am I doing 'ere?"

"What I mean is you haven't bothered your arse in the last seven years so why now?"

"Jim you're gonna be out of 'ere soon so water under the bridge bury the hatchet and all that old shit. I thought we could do something we've never done before."

"What's that then?"

"Talk, and maybe start to build a few bridges."

"Build a few bridges, yeah you could build a few bridges with seventy-five grand couldn't yer?"

"I don't want your money son, you deserve every last penny of it all I ask Jim is you hear me out."

"I'm listening."

"Jim, when your Mum first came to see yer, what was it three or four years ago?"

"Three."

"Yeah three years, well that's how long it's taken me to think about what you said to her and actually admit to myself that you were right and trust me Jim I ain't proud of it."

"What was that then, remind me, I can't remember what I said three days ago let alone three fucking years."

"You reckoned me and your Mum were so heavy on you and your sister coz we were plain fucking jealous, were your exact words."

"Yeah that's right you were."

"Sitting in that cell Jim you had all the time in the world to work that one out and come to that conclusion. I've no doubt you've done a lot of soul searching and wish things could've been different. Well so 'ave I son, you see to me life is just black and white son, I've just got on with it. I never felt I had to question it but you ending up in 'ere and your sister getting pregnant, I suppose I should of coz somewhere down the line me and your mother fucked up."

"Well that's it, it ain't black and white, there's a lot of grey areas in there."

"To me life is, you're a kid, you go to school, you leave get a job or in my case you go and fight a war, you meet a girl, get married and have kids."

"Then you turn into a piss head and become a right miserable bastard."

"Is that how you saw me?"

"Yeah that's about right, I mean when did you ever show an interest in anything I done, all you ever did was slag me off, the music I listened to, the clothes I wore. Not once did you ever pass comment on how smart I looked, I'd spend a fortune on a new suit but you didn't give a shit, it was too much effort to pull yourself away from the poxy tele. You'd just sit there getting pissed till eventually you'd fall asleep or pass out, and then the highlight of your night was waiting for me to get in so you could 'ave a go at me when the only thing I was guilty of was 'aving a good crack with my mates. If you'd took the time to actually talk to me and try to understand what I was all about, you might not of agreed or liked it but at least you would of actually known me, or was that all part of the jealousy thing?"

"Yeah, yer right and as I said I hold my hands up to it, I should of shown a bit more interest but it works both ways son. I can remember on several occasions I tried talking to you about some of the things I went through during the war and how tough it was, perhaps if you'd actually made an effort to listen to me you might of understood me a bit better."

"What was there to understand, I know all about the war, the Blitz, gas masks, ration books, flying bombs, evacuation, air raid shelters and all that shit. I've no doubt it was fucking horrible but that's even more reason to forget it and look to the future, instead of being jealous and resentful and feeling sorry for yourself. You should have been happy for us that we didn't 'ave to go through all that shit. Charlie's old man was the same, he even locked his scooter in the garage and wouldn't let him out after Hastings."

"Yeah the seaside battles, do you expect me to understand that?"

"Yeah I do, as it goes you and your generation were partly to blame for that."

"You what?"

"Yeah, we heard so many war stories from you miserable old gits, it sounded like a fucking laugh so we re-enacted 'em down on the beach."

"You little shit, do you call watching yer mates get their brains blown out a fucking laugh, we fought for our queen and country not a fucking laugh."

"Calm down, calm down I'm winding you up, you're right though it was a laugh, and before you go on about how we fucked up everyone's day at the seaside, that's bollocks, in fact we probably made their day judging by the size of the crowds watching."

"I doubt that."

"It's no different when two geezers 'ave a ruck down the pub, you all want a fucking good look, same as a car crash, you don't want there to be a crash but when there is you 'ave a good look, it's human nature ain't it? Look Dad, we can keep going on about your generation and mine till the fucking cows come home, it ain't gonna make any difference, just accept it. I've no doubt if Granddad was still around he'd tell us that your generation were little fuckers and before his they were shoving kids up fucking chimneys. Times are changing, when young Steven is a teenager he'll probably be getting up to all sorts of shit that I didn't. That's life, accept it, be happy that life's getting better, stop being so fucking bitter and angry and stop living in the past, it's the only way we can move on."

"Yeah your right Jim and when you get out it'll be a new start."

"You still working for the council?"

"Yeah, I'm a manager now."

"About fucking time, how long you been there, thirty odd years ain't it?"

"Twenty-five actually."

"Sod that."

"What do yer mean sod that, it's a good safe job, you could do a lot worse than working for the council, in fact when you get out I'll see what I can do about getting you a start."

"Thanks, but no thanks."

"It's not gonna be easy getting work with your record Jim."

"Yeah, you're right but with seventy-five grand burning a hole in my pocket I really don't give a shit."

"No I don't suppose you do, but it won't last forever, eventually you'll have to find something."

"Yeah whatever, so what's the new addition to the family like then?"

"Steven, he's a great kid, me and yer Mum are gonna miss him when Sarah moves away."

"What do yer mean move away, Mum's not said anything."

"No she wouldn't, she still thinks it ain't gonna happen but I was chatting to Sarah's fella the other day and they hope to be gone after Christmas."

"Where're they going then?"

"Stevenage New Town."

"Why?"

"His family's been up there for the last two years and Sarah loves it, there's plenty of work, the schools are better, if I was in her position with a young kid I'd probably do the same."

"Who's this bloke she's with then?"

"I don't know much about him, he seems a nice bloke, she's lucky to have him."

"Why's that then?"

"Well there ain't many blokes who'd take on someone else's kid, are there?"

"True."

"At least you'll 'ave your room back."

"So after all the shame I've brought on the family I'm s
welcome back am I?"

"To be honest I think the neighbours had more to say about Sa
getting pregnant at seventeen than you getting banged up, with y
they expected it, you were always a little fucker."

"I weren't that bad".

"Yeah you were, how about that time you whacked that 1
around the head with a cricket bat, you nearly killed the poor sod."

"He deserved it."

"Jim, laughing at you coz you were out for a duck don't jus
knocking him out with a cricket bat, or the time you smashed all
windows on old Albert's greenhouse and then there was the time y
set fire to Reg's shed, shall I go on?"

"No, fair comment I was."

"Anyway Jim, I don't give a toss what anyone thinks, you're m
than welcome back."

"Well that's nice to know."

"You any idea what you wanna do when you get out?"

"Everyone keeps asking that but I ain't got a fucking clu
know one thing I won't be picking up where I left off that's
sure."

"You couldn't if you wanted to, eight years is a long time, peo
and places change, look at us, who'd thought we'd actually sit and h
a chat for twenty minutes without being at each other's throats."

"Twenty minutes, they'll be kicking you out soon, well I'm g
you came, you gonna come again?"

"I doubt it Jim, I've said what I wanted to say, I'll let your mot
do the visiting and Jim, don't mention to her about Sarah movin;
don't wanna ruin Christmas for her."

"Yeah, no problem."

"Right I'm off Jim, you've only got another 18 months to go,
and stay out of trouble."

"Dad I appreciate you coming, take care."

"You too, see yer later."

Well that visit from my Dad completely threw me, I was not expecting it to go like that. Mum was right, he had changed. I know it was only a thirty minute chat but trust me that was a major achievement for us. I had no definite plans what I was gonna do when I got out but the one thing I was sure of was I wanted to get as far away from him as possible. I was gonna make a new start; at least now there's no immediate panic, I can stay at my Mum and Dad's place till I decide. The next 18 months dragged by but eventually it was my turn to gather up my few belongings. Nick popped by to wish me luck.

"Jim you old tosser, you're leaving us."

"Yeah at last, thank fuck for that, it seems like a lifetime I've been in 'ere."

"Stay out of trouble Jim, I don't wanna see you back in here and remember what I said."

"What, about getting out at the first opportunity?"

"Yeah."

"Look mate when Mr Warrren came to see me he made it very clear that our paths won't cross again so I can't get out of something I'm not in."

"He came to see yer, what, 'ere?"

"Nah he popped in to see me when I had a weekend off at the country club, of course it was here you prat."

"Well fuck me you were honoured, I've never known him to visit anyone before."

"Yeah we had a chat for about 15, 20 minutes and he's given me..."

"Whoa, whoa, whoa stop there I don't wanna know and you'd do well not to go mouthing it off to every Tom Dick and Harry either."

"Let's just say I ain't got too much to worry about for a while."

"Good Jim, glad to hear it, now you go and 'ave a good life mate."

"I will, cheers Nick."

Seeing that cell door slam shut for the last time was a great feeling but not half as great as walking out them big wooden gates and seeing my Mum and Dad standing just fifty or sixty feet away on Du Cane Road waiting to take me home. We weren't the sort of family that showed our feelings very well. There was no big hug from my Mum, just a beaming smile and a handshake from my Dad that nearly bust every bone in my hand, so I guess they were pleased to see me!

"Come on Jim jump in."

"Nice motor, yours is it?"

"Course it's mine, you like it?"

"Yeah what is it?"

"It's only a Ford, it's a Cortina 1600E."

"Very nice. It's a lot better than that old Popular you used to 'ave, wood trim and leather as well."

"The wood's real, the seats are plastic though."

"Still it looks good."

"Yeah it's the top of the range."

"Yeah he had to 'ave the flashy wheels and bit of wood inside, that's where you get it from."

"What's that then?"

"Being a flash git, you're as bad as each other."

"Jim when you was a nipper how many times did we go past this old prison on the bus and how many times did I say to yer you don't wanna end up in there son?"

"Practically every time, I always wondered what it was like in there, fuck me I never thought I'd spend five years finding out."

"Right, before we go any further can we 'ave a little bit less of the colourful language, you're not mixing with low lifes now."

"Jim do you fancy coming up the legion tonight for a few beers?"

"Your 'aving a laugh ain't yer?"

"What do yer mean 'aving a laugh?"

"Right Dad now think about it, I've just spent eight years banged up with a load of ugly boring old farts, what makes you think I'd want to spend my first night of freedom mixing with another lot?"

"Sod yer then."

"He's got a point love."

"So what you gonna do then?"

"First things first, I wanna get home, 'ave a nice mug of tea, pick my bank book up, get some cash out. Next stop is Tony's to get my hair sorted out then I need to buy some new clobber. Don't worry 'bout dinner Mum, I'll bring some fish and chips in, then I'll give the lads a bell and head off up the West End, get seriously pissed and do some real partying."

"In other words, pick up where you left off."

"Not quite but somewhere along them lines yeah."

"Well you seem to 'ave it all sussed, I hope you're not disappointed son."

"Why would I be?"

"You can't just pick up where you left off, eight years is a long time, I know Ron and Charlie are still about but I ain't seen your mate Dave for a while."

"I ain't too worried about Dave, the last time I saw him we didn't exactly leave on the best of terms."

Well if you're stuck for somewhere to go, the offer stands."

"Yeah cheers."

The journey home took about fifteen minutes but it seemed to take forever. It was strange making small talk with the old man; it was the first time I actually felt on the same level, he talked to me and not at me like I was a little kid but then that was it, I weren't a kid no more, eight years is a long time. We finally got to the house, I stood outside, nothing looked any different, Mum still had the same net curtains. It seemed only yesterday that I was walking down that path and packing my gear on my scooter.

Well, I walked in the living room and there they all were, aunts, uncles cousins the lot, all sitting round eating cucumber sandwiches and no doubt talking about the good old days. It reminded me a bit of a funeral wake; if it weren't for the fact Ron, Charlie and Judy didn't suddenly appear from the kitchen I swear I would've turned round and walked out. Well I stomached the whole Jimmy it's so nice to see yer charade for about two hours. It was driving me fucking nuts so I grabbed Charlie, Ron and Judy and we shot off down the tavern.

"Right now we've got away from that fucking lot what's been going on, who's done what and where?"

(Judy) "You ungrateful git, that lot have taken time off work to welcome you home."

"Look when I was banged up and I could have done with a bit of company not one of 'em bothered their arse to see me and most of 'em are only a couple of stops away on the bus. No, fuck 'em, they don't give a shit about me they're just sniffing around to see what's in it for 'em."

"What do you mean?"

"I'll explain later, so Charlie me old mate how's life been treating you, you still living at home with the old man?"

"Not exactly."

"I don't blame yer, from what I can remember he was a right miserable bastard, I never forget that time he locked your scooter up we hadn't seen yer for so long we thought you'd been abducted by aliens or something!"

"When I say not exactly I mean I'm still at home but I'm married now, the old man died."

"Sorry mate I didn't know, still look on the bright side he won't be locking you up anymore."

"Yeah that's some consolation you prat."

"Alright calm down."

(Judy) "Jim, the funeral was yesterday."

"Oops."

(Ron) "Fucking oops, that's all you can say."

"Well what do yer want me to say."

"Try showing some compassion you heartless fucker."

"Charlie I'm very sorry to hear of the recent death of your beloved father, he was such a caring happy devoted father to you and husband to your mother, the world will be a much emptier place without him."

(Charlie) "Now you're just taking the piss, you're right though he weren't the greatest dad in the world but you're going back eight years Jim. If he'd snuffed it eight years ago, I'd probably put the fucking flags out and had a party but he changed and in the end I got on alright with him."

"Yeah you're right there, even my old man seems a different bloke, so I'm forgiven, am I?"

"Yeah you weren't to know."

"Thank fuck for that, right lets start again, Ron, how's life been treating you, has your brain developed and got any bigger over the last eight years?"

"Bollocks!"

"No come on mate I'm only joking, but let's be honest you was never the sharpest tool in the box was yer?"

"Er, who's got a successful building firm and who's just done eight years?"

"Yeah but to be fair that weren't down to a lack of brain cells just a bit of bad luck."

"Yeah whatever, so now you're out what's your plan?"

"I don't know, perhaps I'll come and work for you. Charlie what you laughing at?"

"Successful building firm my arse, there's you, your uncle and your dipstick cousin fitting the odd bathroom or kitchen, and a bit of painting and decorating, it's 'ardly a thriving business is it?"

(Jim) "Hang on a minute, Ron you don't 'ave to answer to anyone do yer, you're the boss right."

"Yer that's right."

"I take my hat off to yer then, you've done well, I tell yer what I'm not sure what I'm gonna do but I tell yer something, I ain't gonna work for a bunch of cunts like I did before, I'm gonna be the boss."

(Charlie) "The boss of what?"

"I don't know, I ain't figured that one out yet."

(Judy) "Positive energy, stay positive and you'll get what you want."

"Er, yer right, what the fuck you going on about, you ain't turned into a fucking hippie 'ave yer?"

(Ron) "Sounds like it to me."

(Judy) "Everything happens for a reason, sometimes good, sometimes bad but it's all part of your destiny, your journey. For some reason you spending eight years in prison will in some way enhance your life and you'll be grateful for it."

(Charlie) "I don't know 'bout hippie, more like a fucking religious nutter, you ain't joined one of them weird religious cults have yer, them Yanks are well into all that shit."

"I'm not a hippie or a religious nutter, I've just opened my mind to the teachings of Buddah."

(Ron) "Who the fuck's Buddha?"

(Charlie) "He's a big fat Chinese god ain't he?"

"No, no he's not and as much as I'd like to give you retards a philosophy lesson, I'm sure Jim's got other ideas on how he'd like to spend his first day of freedom, ain't yer Jim?"

"Yeah I thought we'd go up the West End tonight."

(Charlie) "Can't mate I've gotta be up at five."

"Up at five, what's that all about then?"

"It's called earning a living."

"What you doing then?"

(Ron) "He's in the same game as me."

"Yeah that's right, difference is though I actually build and I get double what you get."

"True, but I ain't gotta go to beddy byes early and get home late fucked, and I ain't got some nutty fucking paddy on my case all day."

"I'm working on these new towns Jim, that's where the money is, there's shitloads of work."

"Where you off to tomorrow then?"

"Stevenage."

"That's where Sarah has moved out to."

(Judy) "Why weren't she at your little welcome home party?"

"Well she's got the nipper and apparently he's a clever little fucker and they don't want him sussing out Uncle Jim's a naughty boy, they told him I lived in Australia. Charlie, you up there next week?"

"Yeah, why?"

"Well I was thinking of popping up there to see 'em, you can give us a lift."

"I drive a van not a fucking taxi."

(Ron) "Yeah, Murphy's van and he ain't gonna let you waste precious fuel and time doing a mate a favour."

"Yeah he's right Jim, he's a right miserable fucker, anyway you'll be better off jumping on a train, it's only forty-five minutes out of Kings Cross."

"Na fuck that, it ain't worth the risk, I'll get the old man to run us up there."

(Judy) "What you on about risk you daft git, trains are perfectly safe."

"I ain't worried 'bout it crashing, it's just that the last two journeys I've made by train 'ave ended in disaster so I think I'll steer clear of 'em thank you very much. So it's just the three of us then?"

(Judy) "Two actually, I'm flying back at twelve."

"You're fucking joking."

"I wish I was, I fancy a good night out but I've already extended my stay so I could be here for when you got out."

"And there's me thinking you flew back just for me."

(Ron) "That's alright, we'll still 'ave a good crack."

"Yer, fucking great."

"Fuck yer then I'll stay in."

"I didn't mean it like that you prat, course we'll 'ave a good crack, it's just that I expected my first night of freedom being a bit more."

(Charlie) "What did yer expect Jim, did yer think all the old crew would still be around, did yer think we'd all jump on our scooters and ride around looking for a party to crash."

"Course I didn't, but I expected more than just the three of yer, I mean where is everyone, where's Dave, Bunny, Rudy, John, Jeff, Chris and Tony, surely some of 'em are still about?"

(Charlie) "Well Dave and Bunny got married and the last I heard was they were into all that hippie shit, you know free loving and all that. They met some old couple and ended up living with 'em somewhere down in Kent in a big posh house."

(Ron) "Yeah that's right, I was talking to Dave's cousin Steve, he reckons they're into all that wife swapping."

"Wife swapping, what the fuck's that all about then?"

"Well what they do is they all go round someone's house, 'ave a bit of a party, get pissed then at the end of the night they all chuck their car keys in a hat, the wives take it in turns to take a bunch out and whoever's keys they get, they end up shagging 'em."

"Fucking 'ell that sounds alright."

(Charlie) "Na fuck that, knowing my luck I'd end up with the pig."

"Well I can't say I'm surprised, Bunny did like putting it about a bit."

(Judy) "You're not wrong there."

(Charlie) "Rudy progressed from selling uppers and downers to the hard stuff and he ain't been seen for a good few years, rumour has it he pissed off one of the big boys."

(Ron) "Yer that's right, I reckon he's probably at the bottom of the Thames."

(Charlie) "He wouldn't be at the bottom would he, you float to the top don't yer?"

"Not if they tied some bricks round him."

(Jim) "Poor Rudy."

(Judy) "I don't feel sorry for him, he deserved it."

(Charlie) "Yeah she's right, he turned into a bit of a nasty fucker. John's still about, he'll get up here later."

"What about Jeff?"

"He 'ad a right result, you know he worked at the printer's with his uncle."

"Yeah."

"Well his uncle snuffed it and left it to him."

"He always was a jammy fucker."

"That's not all, after a year he sold it to developers, he made a fucking fortune and ended up moving down to the south coast somewhere."

(Judy) "Right, time's getting on, if I'm gonna be back here later I need to get back to the hotel to get my stuff together. How about I meet you back here at about eight and I can have a couple of drinks before I go?"

"Sounds good to me, I've got stuff I gotta get sorted, Charlie, drop us in town mate."

(Ron) "Back 'ere at eight then, see you lot later."

A night up the Railway Tavern, not exactly what I 'ad in mind for my big night out but faced with the alternative of going up the Legion with the old man, I suppose it would 'ave to do! Who knows, perhaps Charlie was winding me up and the old crew are still about and they've laid on a bit of a do for me? I mean things ain't exactly gone how I thought they would so far, I don't know what that big 'welcome home Jim we've missed you so much' load of bollocks was all about, half of 'em I hadn't seen since my auntie Pat's wedding and that was when I was fifteen! But there they all were welcoming me back like I was the second coming of the fucking Lord, but there you go.

It's amazing how the sniff of a few bob brings 'em all out the woodwork, coz I guarantee they all know 'bout my money. Mum could never keep her gob shut. Well they can all go and fuck 'emselves coz it's not like I won the pools, I lost five years of my life for that. Well I didn't know what the plan was for the night but one thing's for sure, I weren't spending all night in the Tavern, so I got my hair done and bought myself a new suit, it looked the fucking nuts! The old man weren't too 'appy when I strolled in at seven but thankfully a few of the old wrinklies were still there so he had to bite his lip and not 'ave a go.

(Dad) "So, where you off to tonight?"

"I don't know yet, I'm meeting Ron and Charlie up the tavern at eight and we'll decide from there. I don't think it'll be a late one though, Charlie's gotta be up at five and I don't fancy a night with just me and Ron."

"Judy not going then?"

"She is but she's gotta fly back later so she's just popping in for a couple of hours."

"We're popping out for something to eat, you coming?"

"Nah I ain't got time."

(Mum) "You gotta eat."

"I 'ave, I 'ad some fish and chips earlier."

"Right we're off, you 'ave a good time, and try to stay out of trouble."

"That I can guarantee."

It felt strange being back home and getting ready to go out. Mum and Dad 'ave changed a lot, thankfully for the better. The house doesn't seem a lot different from when I last saw it, apart from my bedroom, that is. Instead of pictures of gorgeous girls and newspaper cuttings on the walls, it was now a sickly blue with fucking aeroplanes everywhere!

It felt good being back in a suit, if you look good you feel good and although I say it myself I looked fucking 'andsome! I didn't know what to expect when I got down the Tavern, I was hoping that all the old faces would be there and we'd all get pissed and hit one of the clubs. Sitting in that cab heading for the Tavern I was thinking, what if it's just the three of us? I mean 'ere I am all suited and booted looking forward to a right good piss-up with my mates and there might not be any. They might be all married off and turned into a load of boring farts. I might be going to a club on my own and that ain't gonna be much fun propping up a bar on my own, looking like some sad 'Billy no mates'. I got to the Tavern for 8.30, I thought if I was gonna get the big welcome they'd all be in there by then. Well, I've walked in the bar and the first thing I see was Bunny sitting there looking as gorgeous as ever even though it was eight years ago I last saw her and she was partly to blame for me getting so fucked up. She still had an instant affect on my heart rate. I then took a quick look around and there they all were: Charlie, Ron, Dave, John, Judy and Tony!

(Dave) "Come on Jim get that down yer neck, you got some catching up to do, we've been in 'ere since seven."

"Cheers mate, aarh that felt good, whose round is it?"

(Judy) "Slow down Jim you've got all night!"

"Yeah, I will when I've caught up with you lot, I thought we were meeting at eight?"

"We did, Dave got here ten minutes before you."

"Nice to see you ain't changed Dave, you tosser!"

That was typical Dave, always competing, out of all of 'em Dave was probably my best mate but for some reason he felt he had to be better than me. He'd get his scooter to go faster, he'd wait until I picked my suit up then he'd try and get a smarter, bit more expensive one. When it came to crumpet, if I tried pulling a bird and she blew me out, Dave would be in there like a shot and here he is after just ten minutes, trying to drink me under the table and wind me up!

(John) "Jim, sit your arse down and tell us all about your little holiday at Her Majesty's Pleasure."

"It was 'ardly a fucking holiday was it."

(Tony) "Yeah my brother done two years in Wandsworth, he had the shit kicked out of him on more than one occasion, he said it was fucking horrible."

(Bunny) "Well that obviously didn't happen to you Jim."

(Dave) "Why's it so obvious then."

"You've only gotta take one look at him, he's as handsome now as he's always been."

"I don't know 'bout that mate but you've put on a few pounds."

(Bunny) "I quite like it, it suits yer."

"I might have put on a few pounds but I look a lot better than you, you look like how I'll probably feel tomorrow, fucked!"

(Bunny) "Yeah you are looking a bit rough love."

(Dave) "Yeah you're right, abusing life's little pleasures has taken its toll, let's face it Jim the only oats you've been getting are in your porridge, unless of course you bat for the other side! Now, eight years is a long time to go without one of life's greatest pleasures, fucking 'ell I struggle if I ain't had a shag in eight hours!"

"Well it's nice to see you ain't changed, you're still a horrible crude fucker."

(Bunny) "Take no notice of him Jim, he's winding you up."

(Ron) "That sort of thing went on in there then?"

"What sort of thing?"

"Blokes shagging blokes."

"Yeah it probably did but the only geezer I fucked was the Geordie bloke I launched down the stairs, which well and truly fucked him, he snapped his fucking neck."

(Charlie) "Yeah, what was that all about, I heard he tried stabbing yer."

"No not me, he stabbed Mr Warren but before he could finish him off I threw him down the stairs didn't I."

(John) "So you end up doing another five years for saving some arsehole that probably deserved to be stabbed anyway."

(Tony) "Fucking idiot."

"I suppose when you put it like that it does sound pretty stupid, but there was more to it than that."

(Dave) "It don't matter whatever way you put it, it sounds pretty fucking daft to me, who was this Mr Warren anyway, yer boyfriend or something?"

"I tell yer what, if it weren't for him I wouldn't of lasted six months in there. He was like the top bloke inside and from what I've since found out he's one of the top blokes outside as well, apparently he owns half of fucking London."

(Charlie) "Would this be the same Mr Warren who owns Warren's Bookmakers?"

"Yeah he does own a few."

"A few, he owns the lot, he must be fucking loaded."

(Ron) "Yeah he takes a small fortune off you every week."

"When you earn a fortune you don't mind losing a small one do yer?"

"You finally admit you lose then."

"Not all the time, over the year I probably break even."

(Dave) "What a load of bollocks."

"No it's not."

(Ron) "So why is he living in a fucking great house and driving round in a Roller and you're working your arse off and you ain't got fuck all."

(Dave) "Sounds like you've got a bit of a problem Charlie me old mate."

(Bunny) "This Mr Warren bloke, he must have been pretty grateful to yer, what's he do, give yer a few bob did he?"

(Dave) "Yeah if it was me I would've seen yer alright."

(Charlie) "So are yer loaded Jim?"

"Well let's put it this way, I won't be building fucking houses in Stevenage or working as a fucking dustman no more."

(Ron) "So how much did he give yer then?"

(Judy) "Jim, give us a hand at the bar."

"What was that all about, you nearly pulled me bleedin' arm off."

"You was about to tell 'em how much you got you idiot."

"No I weren't, I was gonna tell 'em to mind their own fucking business."

"Well I hope so coz if you tell 'em you'll regret it."

"Why's that then?"

"If you had to work all week for not a lot and one of your mates came into seventy-five grand how would you feel?"

"A bit jealous I suppose – so Mum told yer about the money then?"

"Yeah bless her, I think she thought me and you were gonna get together."

"So you don't fancy me anymore then."

"Na, I'm still loved up with Bob."

"That's good, I'm pleased for yer, from what you used to tell me in yer letter he sounds like a nice bloke."

"Yeah he is, you'll have to come over one day and meet him."

(Dave) "Come on, you got them beers in we're dying of thirst over here."

"Alright, alright, you impatient fucker."

(Ron) "Well come on, you was about to tell us how much you got."

"No, I bloody well weren't, mind your own business you nosy fucker."

(John) "Well judging by the cut of that suit and those shoes you've got on you must of done alright, I'd 'ave to work two months to pay for that."

"Right let's get one thing straight, if I was to offer any one of you five hundred grand to do five years inside would any of yer?"

(Dave) "Na bollocks to that I wouldn't last five minutes."

(Charlie) "Yeah screw that, a good looking bloke like me, I'd 'ave all the bum bandits after me!"

(Tony) "From what my brother told me, I wouldn't do five years for all the money in the World."

"Well I did the five years and I can tell yer I got nowhere near five hundred grand so can we drop the subject now, in fact drop the whole prison thing, I'm out now and I just wanna forget about it."

(Dave) "So where we going later, I ain't spending all night in this shit-hole."

"Dave steady on mate, this is Ron and Charlie's favourite boozer you're slagging off."

(Dave) "You serious, you sad gits."

(Ron) "Yer I suppose it is pretty boring compared to what you and Bunny get up to."

(Bunny) "What's that then Ron?"

(Dave) "Yeah, what we meant to be getting up to?"

"All that chucking keys in a hat and shagging each other's missus."

"You what?"

"I was talking to your cousin Steve and he reckons you're into all that wife swapping."

"He does, does he, and you believe him, you know what a bullshitter he is, he's off his head half the time."

"Why would he come out with something like that then?"

(Charlie) "Yer he's got a point Dave."

"Coz he's a jealous little shit stirrer that's why, as usual he's heard a little rumour and blown it all out of proportion."

(Jim) "So come on then, what was the little rumour that made him think you two are into wife swapping then?"

(Dave) "It goes back a couple of years, me and Bunny met this older couple on holiday in Spain and we became good friends. When we got back we kept in touch and they invited us to a party at their place in Kent."

(Bunny) "Hang on Dave you don't have to explain, if they wanna believe we're into all that let 'em, you don't think we are do yer Jim?"

(Jim) "You Bunny, no never, you're as pure as the driven snow!"

(Judy) "Right shall we leave it there then? Dave the answer to your question is no we're not gonna spend all night in here."

"Where we off to then?"

(Charlie) "I thought we'd go to the Ritzy it's probably the best club this side of the water."

(Jim) "I thought you were having an early night?"

"Yeah I was but you know me, I can never resist a good piss-up."

(Dave) "Yeah great but I don't think Jim will be very welcome."

(Jim) "Leave it out, I've only been out five minutes, not even I can upset someone that quick, what you on about?"

(Charlie) "Bollocks, yeah I forgot."

"Forgot what, for fuck's sake?"

(John) "Well, remember the geezer from Brighton, you know the geezer in the Aquarium Ballroom, Mr Ace Face, the one you spent all night trying to copy them dodgy dance moves, the geezer you nicked the Jag from."

"Yeah."

"Well he owns it."

(Dave) "He don't own it, he runs it."

"It doesn't matter whether he owns or runs it he ain't exactly gonna welcome Jim with open arms is he."

(Charlie) "I wouldn't worry, he probably won't even be there."

(Tony) "You're fucking joking, he's there every night, he loves it."

(Dave) "Well we're stuffed then."

(Jim) "No we're not, fuck it let's go, our paths have gotta cross sooner or later."

(Charlie) "You sure Jim, he's a right hard bastard."

"I know, I saw him take out two Rockers in Brighton."

(Judy) "Jim you've just got out, you don't wanna end up back in there do yer?"

"I don't know what you're all worried about, how's he gonna know who I am?"

(Dave) "Well from what we 'eard you introduced yourself then fucked off with his pride and joy."

(Charlie) "I wouldn't worry Jim, he's like a fucking hoover, the amount of powder that goes up his hooter I doubt he can remember what 'appened last week."

(Ron) "It ain't worth getting up there too early, we might as well have a couple more in 'ere. Jim why did yer nick his motor and why did yer wanna top yourself?"

(Dave) "Coz he's a fucking nutter ain't yer Jim?"

(Jim) "No, no I'm not a nutter, granted I was a little bit nutty back then."

(Dave) "A little bit, you was off your fucking head."

"Yeah I was."

(Ron) "So why did yer then?"

(Jim) "I just thought he was a wanker."

(Dave) "If my memory serves me correctly all you went on about when you got back from Brighton was how fucking wonderful he was."

"Yeah that's right."

"Well how does he go from hero to wanker then?"

(Jim) "When I went back to Brighton there he was fixing up the hotel that only a few days ago he was smashing up, it turns out he was some sort of fucking odd job man."

(Ron) "You're joking!"

"No I'm not, I couldn't believe it, there he is, Mr Ace Face doing a job that was fucking worse than the one I'd just jacked in! I was as angry with myself as I was with him, I just lost all respect for him and I wanted to piss him off."

(John) "So what changed your mind, why didn't yer end up topping yourself, you was in a pretty bad way?"

(Jim) "Well I sat on that rock, I threw the empty bottle of gin in and I watched the bubbles coming out as it sank; it seemed to go on forever, I mean it weren't instant, then I remembered when my old man was teaching me to swim the fucker just launched me into the deep end. I nearly drowned, it was 'orrible, I was splashing around for ages before he got me out, and then I started thinking about other bits and pieces of my life and I talked myself out of it."

(John) "In other words you bottled it."

(Charlie) "Yeah, fuck that it takes a lot of bottle to drown yourself."

(Ron) "I think if I was gonna top myself I'd blow my brains out."

(Dave) "You'd fucking miss!"

(Ron) "Bollocks!"

(John) "A train's your best bet, remember that weird kid from school, what was his name, Jasper."

(Ron) "No Justin."

(John) "Yeah him, he jumped in front of a train, my mate works on the railways, he reckons when the train hits 'em they explode, there's bits of meat everywhere!"

(Bunny) "Charming."

(Judy) "Yeah let's change the subject, we're meant to be having a laugh, not deciding how to top ourselves!"

(Dave) "Yeah come on, drink up, let's go."

Halla fucking lullah my prayers were answered, I can tell yer! I was dreading walking in that boozer, but there they all were, even Bunny and Dave, which was pretty amazing considering the last time I saw them was in the Goldhawk Club and they totally blanked me like I wasn't there. You see Bunny was the girl I had the misfortune of falling in love with, she was stunning and still is for that matter.

Practically every bloke fancied her, she was never on her own for long but I somehow always seemed to miss my chance of pulling her. I knew she fancied me coz she was always flirting with me, then came that crazy weekend in Brighton, everyone was there including Bunny and her latest bloke, but for some reason they ended up having a row. He ended up getting off with some other bird and poor old Bunny was on her own for once, but not for long, I saw my chance and I was in like a shot. We'd spent most of the day together, it was great that night we kipped on the beach and that's where I had her, it was fucking amazing. It weren't much fun when we'd finished, two in a sleeping bag was a bit cramped and them pebbles didn't do my back much good. That was the Saturday night; on the Sunday it all kicked off with the rockers, it was like World War Three, there was Old Bill everywhere, we got split up and I ended up getting nicked and by the time I'd gone to court and got back home a few days later she'd already moved on to Dave, hence them blanking me in the Goldhawk and the rest's history as they say. That was eight years ago and she ain't changed a bit, still gorgeous, still flirting, but then I suppose she has changed a bit, I mean she's still with Dave. Normally Bunny's partners only lasted a couple of weeks or in my case a couple of days. Dave's no different either, he's still winding everyone up and judging by the way he is trying to chat the barmaid up in the Tavern that's probably why he and Bunny are still together, they're as bad as each other!

When I think back, was it love or lust I felt for Bunny? When I walked in that pub and saw her there tonight I think it was both. Yep, I'm gonna find it hard tonight and I don't just mean in my pants, it's gonna be hard not to fall for them charms again. John and Tony hadn't changed much, Judy has gone all philosophical and religious, Ron and Charlie seem well wrapped up in work, boring bastards, that's all they seem to talk about, so it's a good job Dave and Bunny did turn up, at least I'll have a laugh with them.

We got to the club at about half ten, the queue was about twenty deep; as it got down to about five in front, there he was at the door chatting to one of the bouncers, the geezer from Brighton, the Ace Face, the manager, owner or whatever he fucking is! He clocked me straight away, now I don't know whether he remembered me or it was the fact that I stood out, coz I was the only bloke wearing a suit. I really couldn't tell but we got in and I just walked straight past him. Dave reckoned he was screwing at me for ages, the club was great but I just couldn't get in to it, there was too much going on in my head. If it weren't Bunny staring at me it was the Ace Face, I just didn't feel comfortable. I was actually stupid enough to start thinking perhaps Bunny does look at me as more than just a bunk up.

All logic had gone out the window, the alcohol had kicked in and I just weren't thinking straight. Charlie, Ron and Tony left early, probably at about twelve, Judy went straight from the pub to the airport. I don't know what happened to John so it just left me, Bunny and Dave. It was two in the morning, Bunny and Dave hadn't left the dance floor all night, fuck knows what they were on. I was past the point of wanting to dance anymore, the club was starting to empty out so I thought I'd have a chat to the barmaid to see if I could find out a bit more about the Ace Face coz it was bugging me how he went from hotel odd job man to running or owning one of the top clubs in London.

"'ere love, who's that geezer over there, the flash git in the suit?"

(Barmaid) "That's Ray."

Yeah Ray, I remember now.

"So is Ray the manager then?"

"Owner love, he has been for the last four years, you're obviously not from round here then?"

"Well I am but I moved away for a while. So what's he like for a boss then?"

Before she could answer I felt someone squeeze my shoulders from behind as they said,

"Yeah he's a great boss, who wants to know?"

I turned round and there he was glaring at me waiting for an answer, but before I could answer him he said, "I know you from somewhere. I never forget a face, so who are you?"

"I'm Jim."

"No. still not ringing any bells."

"'64, Brighton, Bank Holiday."

"Yer I remember, you're the little fucker that nicked my Jag."

"You got it."

"So, what's with the twenty questions then?"

"Well I was just curious how someone goes from a fucking odd job man to owner of a place like this."

At this point I was bracing myself for a good smack in the mouth but instead he asks me what I'm drinking and pulls up a chair. Dave's clocked what's going on and comes over with Bunny.

(Dave) "You alright Jim?"

"Yeah I think so, Dave this is Ray, Ray this is Bunny and Dave."

(Ray) "Bunny, you're quite a mover."

(Bunny) "Yeah I am and not just on the dance floor either."

(Ray) "Really, sounds interesting."

(Dave) "Well if you're alright Jim we're making a move, you about tomorrow?"

"Yeah I'm back home."

"I'll pick you up about 2.00, we've still got a lot of catching up to do."

I couldn't believe it, Bunny just don't give up, she's just met the geezer and within seconds she's giving him the big come on. Dave couldn't drag her out fast enough.

"What's up, Dave a bit jealous is he?"

"Not normally, I mean you can't be the jealous type when you're married to a bird like Bunny."

"No, I don't suppose you can, right where were we, ah yeah you was about to explain to me why you nicked my Jag."

"Well look at you now, how you are now is how you come across in Brighton. You was the Ace Face, the bloke everyone looked up to, so when I saw yer painting doors, potting plants, washing windows and prettying up the hotel that we so gladly trashed a couple of days before, I just flipped."

"Yeah you're right it was a shit job, so what do you think of what I'm doing now?"

"I've been watching you, you love it, and it's what I'd expect a geezer like you to be doing."

"A geezer like me and what's that then?"

"A good looking flash cunt, that's what."

He just laughed.

"Is that how you see me then Jim?"

"Well I don't exactly know yer do I?"

He's expression changed from laughing to psycho in a split second, he leaned forward and snarled.

"No Jim you don't fucking know me, like you didn't know me back in '64 when you had me down as a fucking odd job man."

"I ain't being funny or nothing Ray but that's exactly what you was."

"I like you Jim, you got guts, plenty of guts but not a lot up top, think about it where was I working?"

"The Grand."

"And was that the sort of hotel that you and yer mates stayed at?"

"Nah don't be daft I couldn't afford a cup of tea in there."

"That's right, I worked in a hotel full of extremely rich people who while staying at the hotel weren't staying at home."

"Well they must have tipped well for you to have all this."

"That's a nice way of putting it Jim, I like that. So why haven't I seen you in here before?"

"After Brighton I ended up getting nicked again, I ended up doing

56

eight years."

"That's a bit harsh for nicking my motor?"

"It's a long story I'd rather not go into."

"Another time hey, look I've got to start making tracks."

"I've just spent the last three years trying to work out what I'm gonna do; after coming here tonight I now know, I'm gonna own a club, like yours."

"Why not, right I'm off, if ever you need any advice pop in, I'm always here."

"Cheers."

It was three by the time I'd left the club; my head was spinning, not from the drink, nah it was spinning from a million thoughts swirling round in my brain. There was no way I'd be able to sleep so I took a slow walk home. I got in at about four and would you believe it the old man was waiting up for me.

"Where the hell have you been?"

"The Ritzy, why?"

"Why, it's four in the morning, your Mother's been worried sick."

"For fuck's sake Dad I'm twenty fucking six."

"I know you're twenty fucking six and you can stay out all bleeding night for all I care but you know what your Mother's like, in future just let her know."

"Yeah right."

"Good night was it?"

"An interesting one, I'm off to bed."

"Yeah see you later."

Well nothing changed there, the only difference was the old man weren't pissed and I didn't get a smack round the head. The next day I forgot all about Dave coming round, he nearly took the door off its fucking hinges.

"Alright, alright I'm coming."

"You fucking deaf, I've been knocking for the last 15 minutes."

"I was asleep, I didn't get in till four."

"Four, I thought kicking out time was half two?"

"It was but I ended up chatting to the boss."

"Yeah, what was that all about?"

"Stick the kettle on, I'll just bung some clothes on and I'll tell yer."

"So he does own it then?"

"Yeah he owns it alright, has done for the last four years according to the bird behind the bar."

"What one was that, the blonde with the big tits?"

"Yer that's the one."

"Fucking gorgeous weren't she, I was trying to pull that all night."

"Do you and Bunny ever let up?"

"What do ya mean by that?"

"What I mean is you're like a couple of sex maniacs constantly on the pull."

"I suppose it's what we do best, that's why we do the job we do."

"And what exactly is it you and Bunny do?"

"Well you know I was telling you about that old couple we met on holiday."

"Yeah."

"Well they've got this fucking great ten bedroom house down in Kent. At one time they were fucking loaded but he lost millions in some dodgy business deal. The thing is, this house had been in the family for fucking years, it meant everything to them so rather than lose it they turned it into an exclusive club for the seriously well off."

"Before Bunny jumped in you was about to tell us about the party they invited you to."

"Yeah that's right, well we got down there and it turned out it was full of rich coke heads and yes, at the end of the night they all end up shagging each other."

"What you and Bunny did as well?"

"No course we didn't but that prat of a cousin of mine to

58

everyone we did, anyway the up shot of it is they asked me and Bunny if we'd be interested in working there as party hosts.

"So what's that involve then?"

"Well we make sure everyone gets what they want if you know what I mean."

"No, Dave I don't."

"Drugs, girls, booze, whatever."

"You silly fucker, I ended up doing three years for flogging drugs."

"It's hardly the fucking same as selling blues to kids in clubs is it?"

"No, it's not, from the sounds of it it's a lot worse."

"Alright lighten up, you're starting to sound like my old man, thing is Jim I don't want to end up like Ron and Charlie working my bollocks off all day for fuck all, me and Bunny like to party, come over here look out the window, see that, it's a Mercedes, you ain't gonna drive round in one of them working on a building site."

"Yours is it?"

"No it's Derek's but it's ours whenever we want it."

"Yeah I see where you're coming from, I ain't gonna work for no fucker either, that's what I was talking to Ray about, I wanna own a club like his."

"Dream on Jim, you any idea what something like that costs and more importantly, what's involved in running it?"

"No not really."

"Exactly so, I would think long and hard what you do with that money, I've met a lot of successful businessmen over the years and none of 'em just went out and bought it, they started off small and worked their way up. I tell yer what, why don't you come down next week, you'll love it."

"I probably would and that's why I ain't gonna."

"So what you gonna do, hang round here and end up like Charlie and Ron, Friday nights up your local, fuck that it would bore me shitless."

"As this is only my second day of freedom and I've got a raging hangover I can't really answer that, I'm just gonna chill out and enjoy freedom for a few weeks then perhaps I'll have more idea."

"Jim here's my number any time you wanna pop down give us a bell, I've gotta shoot off now, it's been good seeing you again mate, look after yourself."

As soon as Dave pulled away in his nice shiny Mercedes his number went straight in the bin. He was right, I would have loved it down at his place but I had no intention of picking up where I left off and that's exactly what I would have been doing. No, for now, I'm quite happy to play it safe.

I spent the next couple of weeks hanging round the West End during the day and going to the Ritzy at night. I was hoping I'd get a chance to chat to Ray again but if he weren't surrounded by birds, he was always deep in conversation with some right dodgy looking geezers. Dave was right, it took about two weeks before I was bored shitless. Charlie and Ron were quite happy to work all week then sit in the Tavern all night talking about football. I even ended up going to the Legion some nights with the old man playing fucking darts, how sad is that.

The only place I seemed happy was at the Ritzy, I felt like I belonged there. I think the trouble was at 18, I weren't ready to give it all up, I still felt 18 inside. I'd watch Ray walking round his club like he was a fucking peacock showing off his feathers. He was proud and aloof, he was someone, I wanted that, I always have. I don't want to end up doing a normal job and having a normal life but I don't want to end up inside again either. Good luck to Bunny and Dave, they were having a great time even if it was a bit dodgy.

Although Dave came across as a bit of a Jack the Lad scatterbrain, he was actually quite a clever bloke and what he said about not being able to just waltz into a successful business, it's something you've got to build up, made a lot of sense. He was right about it costing a fortune buying a club around here. I was looking at a few boozers that were on the market and even one of them would have taken the bulk of my money and that just makes me even more curious as to how that flash git Ray come to own that club?

I tell yer what, it was a good job I threw Dave's number away coz if I hadn't I would have been down there on the first train possible. Perhaps, that's it, I need to get away from here. Judy has done it, so has Dave, Bunny, Jeff and even my sister. Judy was always going on about how wonderful America was, so I gave her a call and asked her if she was serious about me going over and staying with her for a few weeks. She was over the moon so I booked a flight, the earliest I could get was a week later. I was well excited, I couldn't wait to tell my Mum and the old man.

"Mum Dad I'm home, you in?"

(Mum) "We're in here."

"Do you fancy a cuppa, I've got something to tell yer?"

(Dad) "Well come on then, what's got you so excited?"

"I'm going to America to stay with Judy for a few weeks."

(Dad) "When you going?"

"A week's time, next Tuesday."

(Mum) "Well that's nice ain't it, you're flying half the way round the bleeding world to see someone you only saw a couple of weeks ago but you can't be bothered to see yer sister who you haven't seen for eight years and your nephew who you've never met, and they only live an hour's drive away."

"Alright, calm down, you're right, give us the phone, I'll call her now, there you go, done, I'm going up on Thursday."

I hate to admit it but they were right, I was bang out of order but the thought of spending a day with my sister just didn't appeal to me. Before I was locked up, I struggled to spend ten minutes with her, it's fair to say we didn't exactly get on. In fact I'd go as far as saying I didn't even like her. Well I got up there Thursday at about half two just in time to walk to the school with her to pick Steven up. It took about 15 minutes to walk to the school and so far, from what I'd seen of the town it looked alright, all the houses were new, everywhere looked green and clean.

"So you like living here then?"

"Yeah we love it, I could never go back to London, it's a dump."

"You don't miss your mates or Mum and Dad then?"

"Na, it don't matter where you go you just make new mates, and as for Mum and Dad I couldn't wait to get away from 'em, they were always interfering. By living up here, I only see 'em once a month and that's enough; talking of mates there's my mate Tracy over there."

"She's a bit tasty."

"Yeah she's single as well."

"Well you gonna introduce us then?"

"Tracy hang on I'll walk up with yer."

"Who's this then, your bit on the side?"

"Na this is my brother Jim, Jim this is Tracy."

"So where you been hiding him all this time?"

(Jim) "I've been living in Australia for a few years, I've just got back."

"You ain't got much of a tan."

"Na the sun didn't come out much where I was."

"Yer right, so you back to stay then?"

"Yeah."

(Sarah) "You still out tomorrow night?"

(Tracy) "Too right, the kids are staying at my Mum's."

"Where you girls off to then?"

(Tracy) The Mecca, you should come."

"I might just do that."

(Tracy) "Right catch yer later and hopefully you as well Jim."

I couldn't believe it, I've been here just over an hour and I've pulled already. The crazy thing was I'd spent the last two weeks practically every night up the Ritzy and didn't come close to pulling once, whatever happens I have got to get up that club Friday night.

"Sarah I quite fancy that Friday night, if me and Charlie come up can we crash out at your place?"

"Sod off, I ain't having you two back at my place pissed out yer 'eads."

"Well thanks a lot."

"No I'm sorry Jim it ain't happening, I ain't having Steven exposed to that, anyway you're better off staying in a hotel, there's one about 300 yards from the club, so you won't have to stagger far!"

"Yeah, how much is that then?"

"How am I meant to know, you can afford it unless you've wasted that money already?"

Well my little trip to Stevenage to see my sister was well worth it and not just because I've got a dead cert Friday night. I actually got on quite well with her and her husband and Steven was a nice enough kid. They seemed to have a good life up there and as much as I hate to admit it I was quite jealous. Seeing them and the way they were opened my eyes a bit. I always hated the idea of boy meets girl, get engaged, get married, have kids, work nine to five, get home, have yer dinner, watch tele, go to bed and the next day it all starts again. I hated the idea but there they were more or less doing that and loving it. I don't suppose it helped much having parents like ours as role models, they never seemed happy, they were always rowing, it was enough to put anyone off married life.

I couldn't wait for Friday night, I was as excited about that as I was about going to America. I only had one problem, how do I get Charlie to stay away from his local for one night? It's hard enough to get him up the Ritzy and that's only fifteen minutes up the road. I popped up the Tavern when I got back and thought I'd give it a go.

"Charlie my old mate how do yer fancy a night out Friday with a guaranteed bunk up at the end of it in a top hotel and the icing on the cake is it won't cost yer fuck all?"

"You ain't back on the gear are yer?"

"No course I'm not."

"Jim, what you going on about?"

"I went to see Sarah today and while I was there I met one of her mates, a really nice bird called Tracy, I reckon I'm well in, thing is they're all out clubbing it tomorrow."

"And you want me to stand in some club all night while you chat this bird up?"

"Come on mate."

"Even if I wanted to I can't anyway, I've got to go down to Croydon first thing to pick a van up."

"I'll give Ron a bell."

"Don't bother he's coming with me."

"Looks like I'll be going on my own then."

"I don't know what you're worried about, you've been up the Ritzy practically every night on your own, you don't need me to hold yer hand."

"I just didn't want her thinking I'm some sad git with no mates."

"That's exactly what you want her to think, she'll feel sorry for yer and be with yer all night."

"Yeah, I didn't think of that."

So it was off to Stevenage for a night out on my own. The club was huge and it was packed out, I got there about half nine. When I say this club was huge, I mean fucking massive, there was the main disco then off of that there was another one called the Patio then upstairs you had another one called the Nocturne which was for over twenty-fives. I spent about an hour just doing one circuit of the place looking for Sarah and her mates, it was a fucking nightmare. I was getting well pissed off and the more pissed off I was getting, the more I kept drinking. It got to about twelve and by this time I'd had enough, I decided to have one more pint and one last look round then I was gonna call it a night. As I turned away from the bar, there she was chatting to some bloke. Now I knew it weren't her boyfriend coz Sarah assured me she was single so I guessed it was just some geezer trying to pull her and judging by the way they were laughing and joking he seemed to be doing a good job, I was gutted. I spent all night in here looking for her and when I find her, some other geezer gets in first. Well I weren't gonna give up that easy, he had to go to the bog sooner or later and when he does I'll go and say hello. Well, five minutes later he goes to the bar so in I went.

"Alright Tracy?"

"Jim I'm so glad you made it, you been here long?"

"Yeah we got here about half nine."

"Quick, grab me and give us a kiss."

"Fuck mine you don't waste no time do yer!"

As I put my arms round her and started kissing her I felt a tap on my shoulder. I've turned round and there's the geezer she was talking to.

"Who are you?" Before I could answer Tracy's said, "This is Jim my fiancé." He then puts his hand out, shook mine and said, "Congratulations Jim, you're a lucky bloke."

"What the fuck was that all about?"

"It's just some bloke I met earlier in the pub, he's been trying to pull me all night, I told him I was engaged to you just in case you turned up."

"What if I didn't turn up?"

"Well then he pulled didn't he, so who you up here with?"

"Charlie and Ron."

"Where are they then, bring 'em over, we're sitting in the corner."

Oh dear, it's started already after just two minutes of conversation, the bullshit, I just can't help myself, as soon as I've had a few drinks inside me it just flows, half the time I don't even know what I'm going on about. If someone asks me something and the truthful answer makes me look bad in any way, without a second thought the bullshit kicks in. Take that opening conversation for example, she's asked me, "So who you up here with?" Why, because no one goes to a club on their own, it's sad, so to stop me looking like a sad git without a second thought I've told her I'm with Ron and Charlie! I've now got to go over there and come up with some bullshit story why they had to leave early and with the amount I've had to drink that's how the rest of the night's likely to go. What I should really do at this point is make some excuse up why I've got to go early, get her number and take her out when I'm not so pissed; the thing is I really like her. I know I've only just met her but there's something about her, not just her looks but something I can't put my finger on, it sounds crazy but I think I love her. I mean it does happen don't it, love at first sight? Right, the plan is I go over there, spend 10 to 15 minutes light conversation, then tell her I gotta shoot off.

(Tracy) "Where's your mates, we ain't scared 'em off 'ave we?"

"No they left about 10 minutes ago, they've gotta work tomorrow."

(Tracy) "This is Deb and Anne."

(Deb) "And you must be Jim, Sarah's brother."

(Jim) "Yer that's right, where is Sarah?"

(Anne) "Steven was sent home from school today, he weren't feeling too good, she rang Brian up to see how he was and apparently he'd been chucking up all night so she went home."

(Tracy) "Silly cow I told her not to ring."

"The joys of having kids hey."

(Tracy) "So what were you doing in Australia?"

"I worked in the mines."

(Deb) "What coal mines?"

(Anne) "That's a bit of a shit job."

"No yer silly cow, if I wanted to dig bleedin' coal up I would've moved up north, no I worked in the opal mines."

(Tracy) "Good money was it."

"Not really but it had its perks."

(Anne) "You must be fit then doing all that digging."

"Well I didn't really do much digging, I was more like a manager, I was involved in the business side of it, and in fact I'm off to America on business next week."

(Tracy) "How long for?"

"Only a couple of weeks."

(Tracy) "Sarah said you weren't working at the moment."

"I'm not, I've just got to tie up a few loose ends then I'm back for good, I was thinking of buying a small pub or club."

See what I mean 'bout the bullshit, fucking opal miner, I don't know where the fuck that come from and by the look on Tracy's face I don't think she believed it for a minute! I had to get off the subject of me before I came out with anymore bullshit lies about my past so I thought I'd have a slow dance then make my excuses and leave.

"Do ya fancy a little twirl round the dance floor?"

"Come on then."

"So what 'bout you then, you know all about me."

"Not much to tell really, moved here from Fulham when I was 10, got pregnant when I was 18, married at 19 and divorced at 22."

"It's well and truly over then?"

"Definitely, we should never of got married but what can I say, we were young and stupid."

"Yeah I know all about that."

"You couldn't of done anything that stupid, look at you now."

"Believe me I have."

"So is that why you ain't got much of a tan then, stuck down a mine all the time was yer."

"Yeah."

"So where did the plumbing come into the mining then?"

"Plumbing?"

"Yeah Sarah said you were a plumber."

"Yeah I suppose I was, I used to be in charge of the pumping, you get a lot of water in mines."

Now I was starting to sound really fucking stupid so I told her I had to get back to London coz I had an important meeting early next day. It's a shame I'm such a bullshitter coz she wanted me to go back to her place for a coffee, but in a way it was probably best I didn't, coz I really like her. A pissed up one night stand could ruin things, instead I arranged to take her out for dinner when I got back from America.

That weekend dragged on, I couldn't stop thinking 'bout her, all the excitement I had for America went out the window that night. Here I am, met the girl of my dreams and I'm gonna spend the next two weeks with bleedin' crackpot Judy, on the other side of the world. Perhaps crackpot's a bit harsh. After all she was the only one to stick by me when I first got sent down and she's always kept in touch so really she's probably the best friend I've got. It's just that since she's got all religious, she's got a bit boring. We had a bloke inside like that, he kept trying to get me to read the Bible, I ended up reading it just to shut him up but I didn't get past the bit about Adam and Eve and how we're all related. I mean how can I be related to some spear chucking wog in bleeding Africa?

America the land of plenty, I've seen it so many times on the tele I never thought I'd end up going there but here I am in the back of a big yellow taxi heading off to Judy's place. She lived just outside San Francisco in a huge house, whatever her other half Bob done he must be good at it! The first couple of days there I was knackered, she introduced me to a few of her mates and as I suspected they were all hippie types, they were very into love and peace and anti-war. Now my idea of a good night out is get pissed, go to a club, dance all night, make a prat of myself and have a laugh. It's what I've always done and I still get a buzz from it and it's how I remember Judy used to be, but not no more. No, Judy's idea of a good night now is staying in and getting stoned; well I'll try anything once and as I've gotta spend the next two weeks with her I never had much choice.

As it turns out it weren't a bad night, it weren't a laugh or wild or fun it was interesting, there was Judy and Bob, Wendy and Phil, Samantha and Dave and a little fat bird called Julie. Basically all we did was smoke dope and get stoned which is a good job really coz some of the crap they were coming out with would normally of pissed me right off and I would've gone into one, stuff about the war and how we British tried to rule the world, which was true I suppose and we didn't do a bad job considering we're only a poxy little island. I soon shut 'em up when I reminded 'em the British ruled a third of this planet; when we do go to war we don't fuck about, we win, unlike the Yanks who are currently getting the shit kicked out of 'em in Vietnam.

As you can imagine this didn't go down too well especially as Julie's brother had just been sent home in a body bag, but to be honest I didn't really give a shit. I was bored shitless within about thirty minutes of conversation, fucking hippies, and what made it worse they were smart arse educated fucking hippies. The trouble with me is, if I start to get bored or I'm not the centre of attention then I either say or do something really fucking stupid and nine times out of ten I end up regretting it. Like the time I dived off a balcony in a club in Brighton, I nearly broke my fucking neck and ended up getting kicked out. I'd had enough of this dope smoking so I started to hit the lagers which when I'm in a bored state of mind is probably the wrong thing to do.

(Jim) "So Julie what was your brother doing in Vietnam, come to think of it what the fuck are you Yanks doing in Vietnam?"

(Bob) "Fighting against communism Jim."

"I don't get it."

(Phil) "What don't you get Jim?"

"I don't get what the fuck it's gotta do with you if a country wants to be communists."

(Julie) "I agree Jim, and so do a lot of the American people."

(Jim) "At least with us British when we built the British Empire we civilised the countries we conquered, all you fucking Yanks seem to be doing, apart from losing, is blowing the shit out of a country for no real reason other than you don't agree with their political choice."

(Phil) "It's a bit more complicated than that Jim."

(Judy) "Right let's stop there, this is getting a bit too heavy."

(Wendy) "Yeah come on let's lighten up man."

(Samantha) "Yeah let's like totally change the vibe, Jim do you like, dig God?"

(Jim) "What do yer mean dig God?"

(Judy) "She means are you religious and do you believe in God?"

(Samantha) "Yeah man what's your scene?"

(Jim) "No I'm not religious and I think the whole God thing is a load of old bollocks."

(Phil) "Old bollocks, I guess that means you don't believe Jim?"

(Jim) "Yeah you guessed right and when you say what's my scene, if you mean how I get my kicks I can tell you something it ain't sitting around with a bunch of doped up hippies talking a load of shit."

(Dave) "Hey man just say what you feel don't hold back, I love your honesty Jim."

(Judy) "That's Jim."

(Jim) "So is that what you lot are into then, God and all that old rubbish?"

(Phil) "Hell no Jim, how do you put it? 'A load of old bollocks', well we agree."

(Jim) "So what's with all the love and peace then?"

(Judy) "Buddhism Jim."

(Jim) "It's the same thing ain't it, only difference is the image of God is a white bloke with a beard and your God is a fat Chinese bloke?"

(Julie) "Jim, Buddha is not a God, we don't pray to him we…"

(Jim) "Hang on a minute stop right there."

(Dave) "Chill Jim what's the problem, what's spooked you man?"

(Jim) "You fucking lot that's what, was that the plan was it, get Jim doped up and when he's away with the fairies talk him into joining your little cult."

(Judy) "Jim you are funny, calm down and don't be such a prat. What Julie was gonna explain to you before you interrupted her was Buddhism is not a weird religion and Buddha was not a God. He was a philosopher who set out to find the meaning of life and by living our lives by what he discovered, we believe we have enriched our quality of life."

(Jim) "So what's the big life enriching secret then coz so far my life's been shit?"

(Dave) "There's no big secret Jim, just simple things like be honest, honesty is the best policy, you come across as a pretty honest straight talking guy."

(Jim) "Well I am most of the time but we all tell the odd porky now and then."

(Dave) "Porky, I don't follow man."

(Jim) "You know, porky pie."

(Dave) "Still not getting it man."

(Judy) "Porky pie lie, it's a London thing Dave, Jim means we all tell the odd lie."

(Jim) "That's right, sometimes you gotta ain't yer."

(Julie) "Like when Jim, when is it a good time to deceive your brothers and sisters?"

(Jim) "Well before I came over here I met a really nice girl, now if I told her I've just done eight years for selling drugs and killing someone she's not gonna want to go out with me when I get back is she, so honesty wouldn't be the best policy would it?"

(Dave) "Yeah man I dig where you're coming from but the chick's gotta know the truth sooner rather than later, coz she'll just like, get the vibe you're lying."

(Jim) "I think she's well and truly got the vibe already."

(Judy) "Why's that?"

(Jim) "Well Sarah told her I'd been working in Australia and when one of her mates asked what I done over there I told 'em I was a fucking opal miner."

Now, Bob who hadn't said a lot up until now just pissed himself laughing.

(Bob) "Sorry man, opal miner where did that come from?"

(Jim) "I don't fucking know I was pissed wasn't I."

(Judy) "I'm not surprised she's got the vibe, you hardly look like a fucking miner. Listen to me Jim, when you get back you take her out, have a great night then you tell her the truth. Trust me, there's more chance of a future with this girl if you're honest."

(Jim) "Yeah whatever, so is that it then, the secret to a happy fulfilling life is just be honest?"

(Phil) "No man it goes deeper than that."

(Wendy) "Jim do you know what Karma is?"

(Jim) Never heard of it, what's that all about then?"

(Judy) "What goes around comes around, if you do good things, good things will come back to you, do bad things and bad things will happen to you. If for example, you stole Dave's wallet, short term you would have gained but sooner or later you would lose more but Dave will get back what he lost. If you wish bad things on someone that don't deserve it then those things you wish will come back on you. As I've said to you before Jim, everything happens for a reason. If something bad happens to you, instead of being negative and down about it concentrate on the positive side and positivity will come your way; if you're always negative then you'll attract more negativity.

(Jim) "I sort of see where you coming from. I'm not convinced 'bout this honesty is the best policy."

(Julie) "What you got to lose by giving it a try?"

(Jim) "The best chance of a relationship so far since getting out."

(Phil) "Hey man if the chick don't dig yer move on, she weren't the chick for you."

(Judy) "He's right Jim."

Well the evening ended on that note and as I said it was interesting and it did make me think. Over the next seven days, we had several more dope smoking conversations and I hate to admit it but I was really beginning to see where they were coming from. Now I'm not saying I'm gonna turn into a fucking hippie or Buddha or anything like that but watching the way they lived and seeing how happy they were changed the way I viewed life and what it's all about.

When I got back home I had a lot of thinking to do. I'd been out for five or six weeks and in that time I realised that everything and everybody had changed. It felt like I didn't belong to any of it, I felt like a complete stranger viewing other people's lives and trying to decide what was for me.

You've got Dave and Bunny (Charlie got it well wrong when he reckoned they were hippies, the only thing they've got in common with the hippies is the free love bit.) I don't care what they say, I bet they like putting it about a bit at them parties but they seem well happy so good luck to 'em. There's Charlie and Ron, now that was the big surprise, what a couple of boring gits they've turned into. In fact they represent everything I don't want, steady job, little wifey stuck indoors while they're always up the pub talking a load of shit about football or whinging about work. Fuck me they ain't a lot different from my Mum and Dad and they're twice the age. Tony, Chris and John ain't a lot better, the more time I spend here the more I realise I've gotta break away before I end up in the same rut. Judy's done it and although it's not my cup of tea, she's certainly got a better quality of life than this lot round here, and then there's my sister Sarah, she's cut her ties completely from here and she's doing really well.

I look at Ray at the Ritzy and that's what I want, I still get a buzz from the music, the atmosphere, but on the other hand I quite like what Sarah's got going on in Stevenage. Confused is an understatement, my head was all over the fucking place. I couldn't get my head straight round here with Mum on me case all the time. So would you believe I only went and jumped on a train to Brighton. I don't know what it is 'bout Brighton but I just feel drawn to it even with the amount of grief I've had from going there. Sitting on the beach watching the waves roll in and out gave me a chance to really clear my head. The one thing that I couldn't get out of my head was Tracy, I thought about her all the time. I'd only seen her twice but there was something there, something special and I'm pretty sure she feels the same. I'm taking her out on Saturday and I'm gonna take Judy's advice and be honest with her and tell her everything.

Going down to Brighton done me good, it gave me a chance to clear my head and think straight. Saturday soon came round and I was on the six o'clock train to Stevenage. I got to hers at about seven-thirty and she was still getting ready.

"Jesus you're a bit keen, I told you to get round for about quarter past eight."

"Yeah well the old man had to go to the East End to pick something up so he dropped me at Kings Cross and I ended up getting the earlier train."

"There's some beers in the fridge, help yourself."

I was only there about ten minutes and there was a knock at the door.

"Jim can you get that, it's Ken my brother, he's babysitting."

Well I've opened the door and standing there in a leather jacket and jeans is Ken Stevens one of my old mates from school.

"Ken Stevens, fucking hell."

"Fuck mine."

"You know each other then."

(Ken) "Yeah we know each other alright."

"I gotta do me hair yet so you'll have lots to talk about."

(Ken) "Yeah plenty, you take your time."

(Jim) "Jesus it's a small world I ain't seen you since…"

(Ken) "August '61."

(Jim) "That long is it?"

(Ken) "Well that's when we left school weren't it?"

(Jim) "Yer your right, what 'appened to yer, you just disappeared?"

(Ken) "Joined the Army didn't I."

"What was it like, alright was it?"

"Nah, I fucking hated it, do this do that, they were a right bunch of cunts, I couldn't wait to get out."

"Yer, sod that I wouldn't of been able to handle it. I couldn't even handle a job as a dustman."

"When I got out I was gonna get in touch but I heard you was a poxy Mod so I didn't bother."

"So you've moved up here as well then?"

"Yeah couldn't stand London any more, it's turning into a right shit–hole, fucking wogs every where, what 'bout you then?"

"Still in London, but I know what yer mean."

"So Jim, what was it like in Australia digging for opals, hard graft I bet!"

"Yeah you're not wrong there."

"Its funny coz I'm sure we stopped sending convicts to Australia years ago."

"Alright Ken keep it down, Tracy don't know yet."

"But she will by the end of the night won't she?"

"Yeah no problem."

"I'm warning you Jim don't fuck her about, she seems to have a knack of picking arseholes for partners."

"So I'm not in the arsehole category then."

"No, no Jim, you're close mind yer but I never had you down as an arsehole, in fact for a little bloke you had a big attitude and a lot of guts and if you weren't poncing about on fucking scooters all the time, when I got out the army we could have been mates."

"I see you're still into all that greasy hair and black leather."

"Bikes Jim, I'm into bikes, I don't give a fuck what I look like, so how come you're taking my sister out?"

"Sarah lives up here, I came up to see her a couple of weeks ago and met Tracy up the school."

"It's funny you taking Tracy out, me and your sister had a bit of a fling when I got out the army."

"When you say a bit of a fling, what exactly do you mean?"

"Fuck mine, what, do ya want me to do spell it out."

"No, I get the drift, when did you get out the army?"

"April why?"

"No reason, so what you doing here then?"

"What I love best, I work in a bike shop fixing 'em up."

(Tracy) "Right I'm ready let's go, there'll be a bus in a minute."

"Ken it's been great seeing yer again, next time I'm up we'll have to go out for a beer."

"Yeah see you later, don't worry 'bout the time."

Well to say the evening got off to a weird start is an understatement. It was nice seeing Ken again but it's a bit of a fucker him being Tracy's brother. I mean when it comes to hard cases they don't come much harder than Ken. When we was at school you always got pushed about by the kids in the year above, it was just the way it was, it weren't nothing too heavy but Ken hated it. One day we was walking home from school and these kids from the fifth year came running up behind us and pushed us straight through these bushes, we landed in this garden. They were pissing themselves laughing and I must admit I saw the funny side of it but Ken didn't, he got up as quick as he went down. I've never seen nothing like it, he went mental, he beat the shit out of the biggest one and the other two legged it. He was right, we could never have been mates back in '64 because you was either a Mod or a Rocker, we hated each other and from the looks of it he still is. It sounds fucking daft but that's just the way it was. Ken was the last person I would expect to meet in a little sleepy town like Stevenage; I mean he loved London, he always said it was the capital of the world. He loved England, he's yer typical British bulldog, he ain't got no time for all these fucking immigrants. It's bad enough he's Tracy's brother but from the sound of it there's a fucking good chance he's Steven's dad. I'm sure Mum said Sarah was four months pregnant when she told her, and she told her the weekend I got done in Brighton so four months of that puts it at the time Ken and her had their little fling, and even though I never had a lot to do with Sarah back then, I'm pretty sure she never put it about much.

The other down side to Ken being Tracy's brother is the fact that if I muck her about he'll probably kill me. He knows all about my dodgy past so the pressure is well and truly on me to impress the hell out of her and use all my charms, coz whatever happens by the end of the night she's gonna know everything. So if the night's a bit iffy she ain't gonna want to see me again after knowing the truth, that's for sure.

The night was going really well, we had a nice meal, went to a couple of pubs and ended up in the night club. We had a lot in common and we were having a right laugh. I could tell she really liked me so at about one o'clock I started to tell her the whole story from when I got on the train to Brighton.

"So there you have, it the truth, the whole truth and nothing but the truth so help me fucking God."

"Oh well we all make mistakes."

"So is that, oh well we all make mistakes it's been nice knowing yer I'll see you around sometime, or is it, oh well we all make mistakes but you're a great looking bloke with a cracking personality and I can't wait to see you again?"

"What do you think?"

"I think it's been a great night and you can't wait to see me again coz you're falling madly and passionately in love with me."

"Not short of confidence are yer?"

"No I'm not but you gotta admit there's something between us ain't there?

"I ain't sure 'bout the madly and passionately falling in love thing but yeah there's something there alright."

"So when can I see yer again?"

"I ain't said I'm gonna see you again, I just agreed there's something there."

"Come on don't wind me up."

"Yeah I will see yer again, not because you're a great looking bloke with a cracking personality but because you're totally honest and straight. When I first met yer I had you down as a cocky bullshitter who'd be good for a bit of a laugh, and I suppose Ken's told yer I always end up with blokes like that."

"Yeah he did mention you've had your fair share of arseholes."

"How about next weekend? The kids are staying at my Mum's so we'll have the house to ourselves."

"Yeah great, so is it back to yours for a coffee then?"

"That's all it will be and all, Ken's very protective."

"I didn't expect no more, trust me."

"Yeah right!"

She was right 'bout Ken, there he was waiting up, so we had a coffee and a bit of a laugh about the old days then he dropped me off at the hotel. Well, Judy was right about the honesty is the best policy thing. It turned out Tracy likes confident honest blokes; well I've never been short of confidence and since my little trip to America I've decided to cut down on the bullshit, well I have where Tracy's concerned anyway.

The next three or four weeks I was up Stevenage all the time, it was costing a small fortune in hotel bills. Tracy didn't want me staying at her place coz of the kids, she said she wanted to wait till we've been together a bit longer before she introduced me to 'em. Well I'd been out for a couple of months now and after observing everyone I made my mind up what I wanted, Tracy was top of my list, everything about that girl drove me nuts. I now know that what I felt for Bunny was lust and definitely not love.

The other thing I was certain about was, I wanted a club. At the rate I was spending money what I had weren't gonna last forever and once it's gone what the fuck am I gonna do, I'd probably end up like Ron or Charlie or even worse my old man, how fucking scary is that. I knew I couldn't afford nothing in London and even if I could what would be the point? I think deep down, as much as I loved the buzz of London there's fuck all there for me now. I decided to move up to Stevenage; even if it went tits up with Tracy it was as good a place as any to make a new start, only problem was it weren't a huge town and they already had a decent size night club.

Tracy came up with the perfect solution, buy a pub, and once I've got used to running it then start having discos in there. It was a great idea coz not only did I have a business, I had somewhere to live as well and the bonus was, Tracy's done loads of bar work so she could help me out. Well the idea was great but the trouble was most pubs were owned by the brewery. There was one pub called the Punch Bowl, Tracy used to work there, she reckoned the geezer who run it was well into his seventies and he was always going on about selling it, so he could move to the coast, so I went down to have a look. To say it was a shit-hole was an understatement: it was about four hundred years old, not too small with just a handful of old boys in there playing dominoes. I got chatting to the landlord and mentioned I was interested in buying a pub to convert to a disco, he reckoned it was a great idea and if he was younger that's what he'd do to the Punch Bowl. He said he'd already got planning permission to extend it on the side but because of his age and the turnover, he couldn't borrow the money to do it. I asked him if he was interested in selling and he said yeah. He gave me a price there and then and I was amazed, it was well below what I expected to pay, so I wrote out a cheque. He got out the deeds to prove it was his and he said as soon as the cheque cleared it was mine. I was well excited, I couldn't wait to tell Tracy but I thought I'd wait till it was definitely mine, then I'd surprise her. I had to tell someone, I was well excited, so I told Mum and Dad. That evening, I couldn't wait to tell Ron and Charlie.

(Jim) "Well lads I've gone and done it, you are now looking at the new landlord of the Punch Bowl."

(Ron) "Punch Bowl, that's a weird name for a boozer!"

(Charlie "Fucking Punch Bowl, where's that then?"

(Jim) "In the old part of Stevenage."

(Ron) "So I suppose you're fucking off as well then?"

(Jim) "No I thought I'd stay here and travel up every day, course I'm fucking off, the sooner the better as well."

(Charlie) "For fuck's sake Jim, it ain't that bad here is it?"

(Jim) "Well yeah it is actually. I never really gave it much thought until I bumped into a bloke I used to know at school, he's moved to Stevenage coz he reckons London's a shit-hole now and it's full of wogs. He's right, you only have to look around the market on Saturday to see that, it's like spot the fucking white man."

(Ron) "Yeah but you've still got your mates here."

"Have I?"

(Charlie) "We're still here."

"Yeah look at yer, a right couple of boring fuckers, all you do is sit on your arses in this shit-hole every night."

(Charlie) "It ain't a case of us being boring fuckers it's more a case of been there, done it, and now we only need it occasionally and not every fucking week, or in your case every fucking night."

(Jim) "And that's the problem mate, I ain't been there and done it. When I got banged up I was only just starting to get a taste for it. You forget you've got eight years on me, who's to say in eight years' time

I'll probably be at the stage you're at now. I fucking hope not but who knows, all I know is I ain't ready for it yet."

(Ron) "Who do you know in Stevenage then, apart from your sister?"

(Jim) "I met this right nice bird called Tracy, it turns out to be Ken Stevens's little sister."

(Ron) "What Ken Stevens the biker?"

(Jim) "Yer that's right."

(Ron) "When you say little, how little?"

(Jim) "She's only twenty-two with a couple of kids."

(Charlie) "So how do you plan to do all this partying while trying to run a boozer and on top of that, have two kids to worry about?"

(Jim) "That's the whole idea of buying my own place, me and Tracy will get it up and running, then we'll get someone to manage it, and as for the kids, her Mum's always got 'em."

(Ron) "So what's this boozer like, lively is it?"

(Jim) "No it's worse than this place but I'm gonna extend it out and turn it into the best club in Stevenage."

(Charlie) "Tell yer what, when you get the surveyor's report back I'll have a look and we might be able to help you out."

(Jim) "What you on about, surveyor's report?"

(Ron) "You did get a survey done on it didn't yer?"

(Jim) "No the price was right so I gave him a cheque there and then."

(Charlie) "You fucking prat."

(Ron) "Fucking hell Jim, buying property ain't like buying a fucking car you idiot."

(Charlie) "What if it's subsiding or falling down?"

(Jim) "Don't be fucking daft, it's been there for the last four hundred years, it ain't going anywhere."

(Ron) "Four hundred years old, and you think the local authorities are gonna let you fuck around extending it, you're having a laugh."

(Jim) "Well yeah I do smart arse. The geezer's already got planning permission."

(Charlie) "Seen that in writing have yer?"

(Jim) "Not exactly."

(Charlie) "So you ain't, and what's more I doubt you ever will coz you don't just fuck around with historical buildings."

(Jim) "What the fuck are you going on about, it's a fucking pub not a poxy castle."

(Ron) "Don't matter what the fuck it is it's four hundred years old so I guarantee it's listed and you won't be able to touch it structurally, fuck me you'll have trouble changing the wallpaper."

Well the cheque cleared and I became the proud owner of the Punch Bowl, the shittiest pub in Stevenage. Ron and Charlie were right, there was no planning permission! The old cunt well and truly stitched me up. While he was sunning himself on the coast I was stuck behind a bar serving old fuckers their pint of bitter and a bag of peanuts. If it weren't for the fact that Tracy was there with me I think I would have slipped into a right downer, on the positive side it gave me a chance to learn the ropes and ease into this pub lark rather than just jump in at the deep end and get stressed out. Like Dave said, you've gotta start at the bottom and build a business up, well you couldn't get much nearer the bottom than the Punch Bowl. The other good thing was it had a decent living area above it so I could finally move out of London.

After about three months I was running it like clockwork and considering it was half empty most of the time there was enough profit to pay me and Tracy a wage, but boy, was it fucking boring. Poor Tracy had had enough and so did I, it was time to do something with it. Me and Tracy had a few ideas but neither one of us new fuck all about decorating and all that sort of shit so I got Ron and Charlie down to have a look. They were right about not being able to do anything structurally but as far as the interior was concerned, we could do what we liked. So we shut it down, gutted it, put a dance floor in and a DJ booth, put mirrors all round to make it look bigger, painted it up and although I say it myself it looked the fucking business. It weren't long before word got round and within three weeks we were packing it out. On a Friday and Saturday we got around one hundred punters in, which don't sound a lot but in a small pub it was well busy. I was amazed at the profit margin there was on booze.

The first year went really well for me, the Punch Bowl was well established, so much so that I got a bloke called Roger in to manage it. I mean, what's the point in owning your own boozer if you're stuck on the wrong side of the bar all night? Fuck that, I wanted to enjoy it like Ray did at the Ritzy, in fact it was Ray who recommended Roger to me. He was a hard looking bloke, not big or anything like that but he just had a look and a way about him that you knew he could handle himself.

Well Roger was doing a great job so it gave me and Tracy more time to spend with each other and as much as I loved the Punch Bowl it was nice to go to the Ritzy occasionally. Ray always made us feel special and we got to know him quite well. It was on one of these nights at the Ritzy that after a few too many drinks, I had a ten minute conversation with Ray that was to change everything.

"So Jim, how's it working out with Roger then, you getting on alright?"

"Yeah terrific, he knows what he's doing don't he?"

"What he doesn't know about running clubs ain't worth knowing mate, he made the Ritzy what it is today."

"So why did yer get rid of him then?"

"You don't get rid of Roger Jim, he'll move on when he's bored, which usually happens when he's taken a club as far as it can go."

"Well he won't be staying at the Punch Bowl for long then coz we've took it as far as it can go already."

"I never had you down as a plodder Jim."

"Plodder, I ain't no fucking plodder."

"I thought you wanted something like this, I thought you was ambitious, I thought you had the drive to go all the way."

"Hang on a minute, we took a shit-hole of a boozer, we not only doubled the profits, we fucking quadrupled 'em, I'd say that took a bit of fucking ambition and drive."

"Yeah, give yourself a pat on the back, you done well and now you're plodding on nice and comfortable, think what the profit would be if you quadrupled the amount of punters you get in there."

"The only way that's gonna happen is if we extend and that ain't never gonna happen coz it's a listed building."

"There's always a way Jim, have a word with Roger."

(Jim) "What's he, a fucking magician as well?"

"Just 'ave a word."

Well the next day, once I'd had something to eat and I started feeling human again, after a particularly heavy session at the Ritzy, I started thinking about what Ray said. I can't believe the cheeky bastard called me a plodder! I tell yer what, if I took him up the tavern on a Friday night and introduced him to Ron and Charlie then he'd know what a fucking plodder was. It weren't until I saw Tracy later that day and told her what he said that I realised what he was going on about. Like she said, compared to Ron and Charlie I ain't no plodder but compared to Ray I am. Not just content with having the best club in London, he's just bought a club in Southend as well.

As the day went on, more of the conversation I had with Ray came back to me, in particular the bit about Roger. I got on well with Roger and all I had him down as was a fucking good manager, not some fucking night club guru, so I arranged to meet him at the club a couple of hours before it opened.

(Jim) "Sit down mate what yer drinking?"

"Not for me Jim, it's too early."

"Actually I'll put the kettle on, I'm still recovering from last night."

"Good night was it?"

"Yeah it was, we went up the Ritzy."

"It's never a bad night up there, we really turned that place into something special."

"Yeah Ray was telling me all about it, in fact that's what I wanted to have a chat with you about, Ray seems to think you can work wonders with this place."

"That depends on what you want and how far are you prepared to go to get it."

"What I want is a club like the Ritzy but I can't see how that's gonna happen round here."

"Why not, you just buy the field next to the car park, extend the club out and make the field the new car park."

"I wish it was as easy as that but it ain't never gonna happen; this place is listed, you can't fucking touch it."

"You can never say never Jim."

"Well I can when it comes to extending this place."

"If I found a way of making this place bigger and increasing capacity from one hundred to six hundred what would be in it for me?"

"You're serious ain't yer?"

"Answer the question."

"I don't fucking know I ain't had a chance to think about it."

"I have."

"And?"

"I'll cover half the cost for a half share in the club, fifty fifty what do yer say?"

"I say if you can pull that little miracle off you've got a deal."

"Well I know what you want but you didn't say how far you're prepared to go to get it."

"Whatever it takes, I'll leave it up to you."

We shook hands and the deal was done. That night I took Tracy out for a meal and told her all about it.

(Tracy) "I can't believe you done that, don't you ever learn."

"What you on about?"

"Don't you ever give anything more than five minutes thought, you've known Roger for a few weeks and you've done a deal that could lose you half the club."

"No I've done a deal that would give me a share of a club with five times the profit I'm making now."

It didn't matter how much I explained it she still thought I was stupid, yeah it's true I don't really know him that well but if he can pull it off I'd be laughing. I think sometimes you've got to go with your gut feeling and not give things too much thought, that's how I felt when I first walked in the Punch Bowl and look at it now. Alright the old git stitched me up but it all worked out in the end, anyway, I weren't too worried, I knew for a fact he was never gonna be able to build onto the Punch Bowl but I liked the geezer and it was just one of those conversations that would be forgotten about a few days later. It just reinforced the fact that I trusted him and appreciated his efforts. How fucking wrong could I be, I stayed at Tracy's that night and in the morning at about 8.00, there was an almighty banging on the door.

"Alright, alright, I'm coming, Ken what the fuck do you want?"

"You're alive then."

"Course I fucking am, what the fuck are you going on about?"

"You ain't heard then?"

"Stop fucking about and tell me what's going on?"

"Well at this moment in time they're sifting through a pile of ashes looking for bits of you, the Punch Bowl, its gone mate, it's completely burnt down along with one of the firemen as well."

"No, no fucking no."

"Yes, yes fucking yes, switch the radio on, it's been on there all morning."

"Fuck the radio, can yer run us up there?"

When I got there, there was old Bill and firemen everywhere; Ken weren't exaggerating, the only thing still standing was the fucking chimney. I made myself known to the police and straight away I was taken down the station for questioning. Even before the ashes had time to cool down the fire investigators knew it was arson and with one of the firemen getting killed whoever done it will be on a manslaughter charge as well. The copper who interviewed me was a Sergeant Dickson and as coppers go he weren't a bad bloke.

"So Jim what was you up to last night."

"Well I weren't torching my club if that's what yer thinking."

"Why would I think that then?"

"Well I don't see anyone else being questioned."

"We'll be interviewing every one connected to the club right down to whoever cleans the bogs, so I'll need a list of everyone connected to the club, but for now I just need to know where you were at around four this morning?"

"I was tucked up in bed asleep, I was out with my girlfriend last night and I stayed at hers."

"She will verify that will she?"

"Course she fucking will."

"Calm down, you've got nothing to worry about."

"I hardly call having my club burnt down nothing to worry about."

"Jim is there anyone you can think of who might want you out the way."

"No, no one, as you know I've only been out just over a year and I get on with everyone, why do you think that?"

"I understand you live above the club and most weekends you're there."

"Fucking hell I didn't think of that."

"So we can rule you out as the target then?"

"Yeah, fucking right you can."

"Has there been anyone you've kicked out or had aggro with at the club?"

"I tell you what, you're better off talking to Roger about that, I haven't been there that much over the last couple of months."

"Who's Roger then?"

"He's the manager."

"I see from your record Jim you're from my neck of the woods."

"Yeah London born and bred, what part you from?"

"The Bush Jim, Shepherds Bush, Rosedean Avenue to be exact."

"Fuck me it's a small world, I lived in Temple Street."

"It's a smaller world than you think Jim, right I'm sure you got lots to sort out so I won't take any more of your time, just let me have that list later and we'll see if we can sort this mess out, and Jim don't worry."

Now I've had my fair share of police interviews over the years but none as easy as that, fuck me he was so nice and polite, I was half expecting him to invite me round his place for tea and biscuits. Something weren't right, don't get me wrong, when I say something weren't right I mean it weren't right in a good way. There's me just got out the nick for drug dealing, vehicle theft, manslaughter and not forgetting the Public Order offences and this Dickson geezer's giving me an easy ride. I tell yer what, I was shitting myself going down that station, with my record I was expecting a right grilling, even though I had fuck all to do with the fire. I had a gut feeling Roger did and trust me, a grilling from a right nasty bastard copper and he would have picked up on that.

I tried getting hold of Roger all morning, I had one hundred and one things I had to do but I couldn't do fuck all till I'd seen him. I gave up trying the phone so I went over the lakes where he spent most of his spare time fishing would you believe. I took a short cut through the woods and just as I was about to go through the opening to the lake I could see him talking to some geezer in a suit. Now this was very strange, you get people walking dogs in their wellies, you get kids mucking about on their bikes, you get romantic couples holding hands and feeding the fucking ducks but you don't get too many suited and booted geezers walking round so I sneaked round the back of 'em to get a closer look. I couldn't believe it, there he was having a cosy chat and a laugh with Dickson the copper!

I couldn't get close enough to make out what they were talking about but judging by the way they were laughing it weren't no interrogation. I felt like my fucking head was gonna explode, how the fuck did Dickson know where to find him? Come to think of it how did Dickson know who he was, I mean I hadn't had a chance to give him the list yet, all I told him was his name was Roger and judging by the way they were acting, they looked like they went way back and if they did why didn't Dickson mention it earlier at the station? There was just too much to take in, now was not the right time to confront Roger so I went back to Tracy's.

"Is everything alright, Ken said you'd gone down the station for questioning?"

"No everything's not alright, Ken was right, there's nothing left of the club, it's well and truly burnt to the ground and the worst thing is it weren't no fucking accident."

"I don't get it, who'd want to burn it down?"

"I hope I'm wrong but I think Roger did."

"Roger, why, only yesterday he was talking about enlarging it not reducing it, it don't make sense."

"Yeah it does, it makes perfect sense, think about it, he was pretty confident he could make the club bigger, we both know he weren't gonna get permission to extend it. Well he don't have to, there's nothing to extend, there is no listed building, all that's there is a plot of land for a new club."

"Shit, you need to talk to him."

"I know, I've been trying to get hold of him all morning, so I went over the lakes where he usually fishes and there he is having a cosy chat with the copper who interviewed me."

"Jim you need to sort this out."

"I know, there's a lot I gotta sort out, like where I'm gonna stay?"

"You can move in here if you want, we've been seeing each other for over a year now and the kids get on alright with yer."

"Yeah great I'd love to, well it ain't gonna take long to move in, all my gear went up with the club."

"Give me some money, I've gotta go up the town, I'll get you a few things to tide you over, while I'm doing that it'll give you a chance to sort things out with Roger."

Sort things out with Roger, that's easier said than done. Now I like Roger but to be honest going to see him scared the shit out of me, more than going down the station. It weren't necessarily Roger that scared me it was what I was getting into, I mean a fireman dead, if I'm connected in any way to that then they'll lock me up and throw away the key. I went back over the lakes and there he was like he didn't have a care in the world.

"Caught anything?"

"Hello Jim, what you doing over here?"

"Looking for you, well actually I knew you was over here coz I see you earlier having a cosy chat with that copper Dickson."

"You mean Stu."

"I don't know, I'm not on first name basis with him, I just know him as Dickson."

"What, you spying on me Jim?"

"No, not at all, it's just that I've been trying to get hold of you all morning so I came over here."

"What's bothering yer Jim?"

"The Punch Bowl, you torched it didn't yer?"

"No, not me, my old Mum always told me you play with fire, you play with the devil."

"Thank fuck for that."

"No I was nowhere near it I was at the Ritzy with you, Tracy, Ray and Ray's lovely girlfriend Melissa."

"What the fuck you talking about, you said you didn't torch it."

"That's right, I didn't say I had nothing to do with it though."

"So who did you get to do it?"

"All you need to know is we spent the night at the Ritzy then we went back to Ray's."

"No that's bollocks I was at Tracy's all night."

"Apart from Tracy, who can back you up?"

"I don't need backing up coz that's where I was."

"Yeah Jim you do, I'll tell you now if the insurance company can't totally eliminate you from any involvement, they won't pay out and trust me an alibi from your girlfriend won't be enough, especially with your record."

"I've already told Dickson I was at Tracy's."

"Don't worry about Stu, it's sorted, he's expecting you in the morning for the official interview."

"Bent coppers, arson and on top of that a dead fireman, I'm sorry mate but I want out."

"The way I see it you've got two options, you can see Stu tomorrow, he'll make sure your statements right, once the old Bill are happy the insurance company will pay out, I'll get the plans drawn up for a bigger better club and in about a year's time we'll be up and running. The up side for you is you'll have exactly what you want, a bigger better club with a huge turnover. The downside is you're in it up to your neck, if it does go tits up you'll be spending some more time at Her Majesty's Pleasure. It's very unlikely it will but there's about a five percent chance it could.

The other option is you tell it exactly how it is, right down to the conversation we're having now and if you really want out I mean you've gotta tell 'em everything. Let's say in a moment of madness you go down that route, how do yer think they're gonna see it? I'll tell you exactly how they'll see it. There's Jimmy, he ends up inside for drug dealing, gets mixed up with the wrong sort inside, ends up killing someone then gets out and with financial help from his dodgy contacts he met inside he buys a club which gives him the perfect opportunity to continue his drug dealing, but he gets greedy and the club's not big enough so he wants to extend it. He can't get permission so he torches it so he can build a bigger one but a fireman gets killed and he panics, so he then makes up this little story about his dodgy bar manager (whose only crime to date, incidentally, is pissing up the side of a police car when he was a teenager) and his bent copper mate who just so happens to be one of the best and tipped to be the next superintendent. Now Jim, who do you think they're gonna believe, me with an airtight alibi or you with your dodgy past and your girlfriend's word? If you take the first option there's the five percent chance you'll shit out and get done, the second option there's a ninety five percent chance you'll get done and lose the fucking lot and when you get out next time you'll be a nobody with fuck all."

"When you put it like that I ain't got a fucking choice have I?"

"Yeah you have, you've always got choices, you choose what you want in life Jim, you came to me Jim, I didn't come to you, I said how far are you prepared to go?"

"And I said whatever it takes, I'll leave it up to you."

"Yeah Jim you did, so what's the problem?"

"The problem is there's two kids left without a dad and a wife without a husband because of you."

"That's bollocks mate, that fireman's dead coz he decided to do a dangerous job, I didn't kill him nor did the geezer who put the match to the petrol. If you decide to fight fires you gotta expect them to fight back. His time was up mate, if it weren't the Punch Bowl fire it would have been another one next week or the week after. I don't feel a shred of guilt and nor should you. Look, if it makes yer feel better we'll donate all the profit from the opening night to his wife and kids."

"I'll clear it with Tracy tonight and see Dickson tomorrow."

"You've known her five minutes, just tell her what you have to."

"Yeah I'll just get the alibi right."

"Right, I've done all I can here, I'm fucking off for a while, you won't need me till you've got the nod from the insurance company. If you've gotta get hold of me, Ray knows how to contact me and Jim, relax mate, you've got nothing to worry about, trust me."

Nothing to worry about, I tell yer, I was shitting myself, I felt like I'd made a pact with the fucking devil. I decided to tell Tracy everything then if it did all go tits up and we all got done my conscience was clear. She really surprised me, I thought she'd need time to think about it, after all it weren't just her it was the kids she had to think of as well, but no she just gave me an answer there and then. She wanted in, in fact she was the complete opposite to me. I mean there's me shitting myself and she, well she just thought it was a bit of a laugh, a bit of excitement she said, and I suppose from her point of view it was. Let's face it there ain't a lot of excitement in bringing up a couple of kids and running a house is there? We gave our statements and as far as the old Bill were concerned we were in the clear, the insurance company though weren't so convinced, in fact the insurance inspector gave us more of a grilling than the cops but then I suppose they would. After all they'd be the ones parting with the cash to rebuild it.

It was just a waiting game now, there was nothing we could do 'til the insurance company were happy, me and Tracy got on great. I weren't that into the kids like she was but then they weren't mine were they? She did mention on a few occasions if I'd like kids of my own and the answer was always a definite no. I just didn't want that kind of responsibility, I liked being an irresponsible prat. A few months had gone by and I was starting to get restless and bored so I started popping down to see Ken at the bike shop for a chat and a cup of tea. It was only a small business, there was just Ken and the old boy who owned it, Ken done all the work on the bigger bikes and John the old boy worked on the mopeds and scooters. I was down there so much I ended up doing bits and pieces to help 'em out, I didn't want nothing for it, I was just grateful it gave me something to do. It stopped me going fucking nuts. Well I popped down there on Thursday like I always did and as I got there an ambulance was pulling away.

"Ken what's up mate, what's happened?"

"It's John, he collapsed."

"What's he have, a heart attack did he?"

"How do I know, I'm a mechanic not a fucking doctor, one minute we were sitting there having a cup of tea and a chocolate biscuit, the next thing his face went all droopy down one side and he started talking like a fucking spastic, then he just collapsed."

"That's what happened to my uncle Bill, he was never the same after that, he ended up in a wheelchair."

"Shit, its serious then?"

"Yeah too right it is, he might not even make it."

"Jim do us a favour mate, get these bikes in and lock up, I've gotta shoot round and tell his missus."

"Yeah no problem, take your time, she'll be gutted won't she?"

"Yeah she will, so am I, he was like a father to me."

As I suspected John had had a stroke and he was gonna be out of action for months. Ken was never gonna be able to run the shop on his own so I started to work there full-time until John could return. The more I got to know Ken the more I liked him. There was no pretending with Ken, if he liked yer he liked yer, if he didn't then you knew it. He liked his beer, bikes, country and more than the occasional flutter on the gee gees, hence he never had a pot to piss in but he was happy. Yeah he was a dirty fucker but he had a heart of gold and for some reason he really liked me, fuck knows why coz we didn't have nothing in common apart from his sister. Well, six months had soon gone by and the insurance company still hadn't paid out. I enjoyed working with Ken but I was itching to get the club up and running. I had hundreds of ideas but couldn't do anything without the insurance money. Poor old John didn't seem to be getting any better and Ken got the news he'd been expecting and dreading: John was selling up.

Well, the bike shop was on the market for nearly four months and there was no interest, so he offered it to Ken at nearly half the asking price. It was an absolute bargain but if it was a quarter of the price Ken still couldn't have got the money together. I thought about it for a couple of weeks then had a chat to Tracy about it and decided to buy the shop. It made a lot of sense having something separate from the club. The club was fine but there was always that dodgy side to it and now Roger's involved anything could happen, whereas the shop was safe. The deal was I gave Ken the money to buy it so it was in his name, he dealt with running the repair side of the shop and I dealt with retail and managing the finance side of it, coz if it was left to him all the profits would end up down the bookies. It worked really well. Ken was happy coz he kept his job and doubled his wage and I was happy coz I had a safety net in case the club went tits up.

Well, after a year of fucking around with the insurance company, the planning department, surveyors, architects and builders we finally got the go-ahead for the club. Work started in August and the opening was scheduled for Saturday June 20th which meant another year in the bike shop. Now like I say, I liked Ken but I swear if I heard him sing be bop a fucking lula one more time I'd put a monkey wrench round his fucking head, and the other thing that was winding me up was constantly having oil and shit all over me. I didn't want to end up smelling like a fucking biker did I, so I decided it was time to get Ken some permanent help.

We started a young bloke called Eddy. Ken got on with him great, especially as his dad had named him Eddy after the old rocker Eddy Cochrane. Well, now we got Eddy on board it gave me a chance to look at the business a bit closer to see how we could up the profit margin a bit. As much as Ken didn't like it, the way forward was selling small bikes like scooters and mopeds. When Ken finally got it into his head that running a business was about profit and not love I stepped back and let Tracy take over. She was great, she run the shop like clockwork; she came from a pretty close family so her Mum and Dad were well chuffed she was working with Ken. They weren't so chuffed however that we'd been living in sin for a year and there weren't even an engagement ring sitting on her finger. I got on alright with her Mum and Dad, they just pissed me off a bit coz they were always having little digs about the marriage thing and I just felt pressured all the time. I suppose the way they saw it was we'd been seeing each other for about two years and living together for a year so we were as good as married anyway, but as good as married ain't the same as actually being married is it, it can't be can it. I mean me and Tracy are well happy, we still go out to clubs and have a laugh, we genuinely enjoy each other's company and we still have sex on a regular basis. How many times can I remember hearing my Mum have a go at the old man coz she weren't getting enough coz he was always too tired? Na, fuck marriage, I think we'll stay as we are.

Now work on the club has started, Roger's back on the scene and we're spending a lot of time together sorting out all the boring shit like décor and who's doing this and who's doing that. It's funny coz when I was working with Ken, while we were waiting for the go-ahead for the club, I was itching to get started and get it up and running, but now Roger's a partner in it he seems to have taken over, and to be honest I've been quite happy to let him; after all, he didn't do a bad job getting the Ritzy up and running. So we had a little chat and it was decided that Roger would deal with the builders and the business side of things and when the club opened I'll deal with promoting it and sorting out entertainment and staff. In other words, Roger got to do all the boring shit and I got all the fun bits, perfect!

Christmas came and went and things were looking great, the club was on schedule and the bike shop was doing well. Now I'd taken a back seat with the club I was spending a fair bit of time at the shop, it was a nice atmosphere there. Tracy had made friends with the girls next door at the hairdressers and they were always popping in. The record shop on the other side was always playing a good mix of tunes so this put Ken off his Gene Vincent impersonations, which was a good thing. Yeah, I always enjoyed popping in the shop and the bonus was we were making good money. Me and Ken got on great in the shop but outside we had totally different ideas on what a good night out was, so it surprised me when he asked me if I wanted to go out for a few beers.

"I'll pick you up at eight then?"

"Yeah right, where're we going?"

"Up the Red Lion."

"You're fucking joking ain't yer?"

"Na, why would I, I'm up there every night, what's wrong with it?"

"Well for a start, it's full of your lot."

"What do yer mean my lot?"

"Bikers, greasers, fucking rockers or whatever you call yourselves these days, it's that fucking dirty in there you wipe your feet on the way out."

"Well I ain't gonna get into one of your poncie clubs looking like this am I?"

"Try having a wash and change your shirt, you'll be alright."

"Bollocks, be ready for eight."

I was not looking forward to our Friday night out. Whenever you go past the Red Lion there's always old Bill or an ambulance outside, but Ken's right, there's more chance I'll fit in better there than he would in one of my favourite boozers. We walked in and it weren't too bad, yeah it was a shit-hole alright and it was full of big ugly bikers but Ken seemed to know 'em all so I felt safe enough.

"So why did you feel the need to bring me to this friendly little drinking hole then Ken? I hope you don't think you can turn me into one of your lot, coz it ain't 'appening, just because I own a bike shop, that's where my involvement ends, there's more chance of me joining the fucking priesthood.

97

"You finished bitching?"

"Yeah."

"What makes you think we'd want a weedy little ponce like you joining up anyway, what you having?"

"I'll have a lager mate, so why am I here?"

"Does there have to be a reason for a couple of mates having a few beers together?"

"No, no I don't suppose there does, it's funny how we are mates ain't it, I mean we ain't got fuck all in common have we, in fact we're complete opposites."

"Yeah, you're right, apart from Tracy and it's because of Tracy I want a little chat with yer."

"I don't like the sound of this, go on chat away."

"Right, how do you feel about her?"

"I'm nuts about her, you know that."

"No I don't, see the way I see it is if you were so fucking nuts about her you'd want to marry her."

"For fuck sake Ken, it's bad enough your Mum and Dad keep going on about it, I don't need you on me case as well. What is it with your poxy family and this obsession with marriage? If you're happy together, what's it matter whether you've got a bit of paper or not?"

"I suppose from a bird's point of view it means security and commitment."

"Yeah and you know what 'appens then once they're all happy, content and secure and they've got that ring on yer finger?"

"No Jim I don't, what 'appens then?"

"Well they let 'emselves go don't they? They start shoving cakes in their gobs, put weight on and stop making the effort, coz they've got yer ain't they, and then what 'appens is you don't wanna shag 'em anymore, so you end up shagging some bird you pick up at a club. She finds out and then you get well and truly screwed coz she gets to keep the house and everything and you end up in digs, and the worse thing 'bout it is, and this is the real killer, she then loses all the weight coz although she's put all the blame on you and you're the complete bastard for shagging the little tart from the club, deep down she knows it's her fault for turning into a fucking heifer. So like I say, she loses all the weight, starts looking gorgeous again, finds some other bloke and lives 'appy ever after. Na trust me Ken, marriage ain't worth it."

"You really do talk a load of bollocks sometimes don't yer?"

"Bollocks is it, well you look at Sarah and Brian."

"You're joking, I thought they were well solid, mind you having a kid that young couldn't of been easy."

"Yeah, especially as it ain't his."

"Well whose is he then?"

"How am I supposed to know?"

"How old is Steve now?"

As soon as I opened my gob and said Brian ain't the dad, Ken's clocked it and his tiny brain's gone into overdrive. I've always been ninety-five percent sure Ken's his real dad, I mean the timing was spot on when they had their little fling, and like I've said before I'm pretty sure my sister didn't put it about too much.

"'Bout ten I think, same again Ken?"

"No, I'll have a dark rum, and make it a double."

I was hoping by the time I'd got the drinks in he'd drop the subject but he was like a dog with a bone.

"So how long was she on her own before she met this Brian geezer then?"

"I don't fucking know do I, I was banged up at the time."

"I've always fancied your sister."

"What, even now she's put on a bit of weight?"

"Well I ain't exactly a featherweight am I?"

"No you're not, yer fat bastard."

"Only you can get away with that, you skinny twat."

"You know I love yer, anyway we're not here to talk 'bout Sarah, I thought we was here so you could lecture me 'bout marrying Tracy."

"Yeah that's right, well to be honest I don't give a monkey's whether you marry her or not but I'm just pre-warning yer, I heard her chatting to that bird from the hairdressers next door, apparently it's a leap year in February and birds can ask blokes to marry 'em, so she's gonna ask yer and that ain't right is it?"

"I had no idea she felt that strongly 'bout it."

"No I don't suppose you did, you're too busy being that somebody you've always wanted to be."

"What the fuck do ya mean by that?"

"You once said to me, "life's fucking boring, you get up, go to work, get home, go to bed and it all starts again, it's all the fun bits that makes life worth living, far better to take a few risks and be a somebody than a boring nobody. I'd rather top myself than be nobody. Well you came close to it and you ended up doing eight fucking years just because you didn't wanna be like everybody else, well perhaps it's time to grow up and be a husband instead of hanging around with those arseholes at the club."

"Them arseholes as you put it are my mates."

"Bollocks are they, they're fucking gangsters and you know it and it's only a matter of time before you end up back inside again."

"Hang on a minute, if it weren't for me doing eight years and all that I wouldn't be 'ere now and you'd be out of a fucking job."

"So you're telling me you don't regret losing eight years of your life?"

"No, no I don't."

"Bollocks!"

"No it ain't, don't get me wrong, when I was inside I fucking hated it, sometimes I wished I'd drowned my fucking self or jumped in front of that train, but as time went on I got used to it and it weren't so bad. Someone once told me everything 'appens for a reason, it don't matter what shit you're going through it's not until later you look back and think, well I'm glad that 'appened, because nine times out of ten you'll find something good came out of all the shit."

"Yeah, right."

"Yeah I am right, I'm glad I done eight years."

"You fucking serious?"

"Look mate, before I got sent down I was in a right fucking state, I worked as a fucking dustman carrying shit around and working with a bunch of sad tossers. Most of the time I was pilled up, I didn't know whether I was coming or going, my Mum and Dad were glad to see the back of me. I tell yer, if I hadn't of got sent down I'd either ended up in a fucking nut house or I'd be six foot under, but look at me now, I've got two businesses, money in the bank, a gorgeous bird. I've got a fucking life and yeah, I'm someone, I ain't just another Mr fucking normal who works in a factory or a fucking building site getting covered in shit every day."

"Yeah I'll give yer that, there's fuck-all normal 'bout yer Jim, but as for being a someone, yeah you are, you're Jimmy, not fucking Al Capone or Ronnie fucking Kray, you're not like them Jim, you're out of your depth and sooner or later they are gonna fuck you over, trust me."

"Na bollocks, you've got it all wrong."

"'ave I?"

"Lecture over is it?"

"I don't give a fuck what you do mate, just remember it ain't just you, you gotta think 'bout it, there's Tracy and the kids now."

"Yeah, you're right there, what the fuck am I gonna do 'bout this marriage thing?"

"You know what I think, look mate I'm shooting off, I don't know 'bout you but I've 'ad enough."

"Yeah fuck it, let's go, this place is making me itch, fucking shit-hole, next time we're going to one of my boozers."

That's what I like about Ken, he don't mince his words, he just says it as it is. Well it was a quick drink and a short night but he said enough to make me sit up and think, am I really just kidding myself, am I like Ray and the others or am I just a fake? I must admit when I was inside that's how I felt, I mean I weren't really a drug dealer was I? I was just in the wrong place at the wrong time, same as when I pushed Henry down the stairs, but looking at what I've got now, I was in the right place at the right time definitely. But Ken could be right, perhaps I'm not like them and if I'm not will they, as Ken put it, fuck me over? Well one thing's for sure, I'll certainly be looking over my shoulder, I don't trust the fuckers. I can handle that side of things but the whole marriage thing freaked me out. If Tracy does ask me and I say no, then that could be the end and I don't think I could cope without Tracy in my life. It's the one piece of normality I actually like. Well, I gave it a lot of thought over the next few weeks and I decided to get in before she could and I proposed, June 20th 1975 was the date, yep, the day the Punch Bowl reopened. Tracy had the right 'ump 'bout that but the way I saw it was, we get married early, do the boring family thing, you know cucumber sarnies, polite chat to all the old wrinklies, then fuck 'em all off home and 'ave a decent piss-up at the club with all me mates, perfect!

The next five months seemed to drag on, I was getting well pissed off with practically every weekend meeting a different aunt, uncle, cousin, fucking granny and granddad. I must have spent more time in that five months with her family then I 'ave with mine in my entire life, but I suppose that's what normal families do, unlike my dysfunctional lot! You see mental health runs in my family, my uncle Sam was always trying to top himself; when he finally did it was a poxy accident, he fell off a poxy ladder while cleaning the windows and broke his neck! Everyone thought I was nuts, I think that's why my Mum and Dad gave up on me and had more time for Sarah. Who knows, perhaps I'm not the full ticket but I ain't done bad so far 'ave I? Alright, the eight years I done was a bit of a shit but look at me now, all loved up and ready to settle down, unlike my perfect fucking sister who got knocked up as a kid and is now heading for the divorce court.

The one good thing 'bout these little family get togethers was Ken was usually there and we'd 'ave a bit of a laugh and normally end up down the pub getting half cut. I got to know him quite well and he was well chuffed I asked him to be best man. He weren't 'appy 'bout having to wear a suit though, but then if someone told me I had to wear dirty jeans and a leather jacket for the day I wouldn't be too thrilled either. I noticed at some of these family get togethers Ken was trying very hard to get to know Sarah, which was quite surprising really. Don't get me wrong, Sarah's nice enough but she's never in a million years gonna get that fat arse on the back of a Triumph! Biker birds, I hate to admit, are usually well tasty in a dirty sort of way. They've normally got lovely little arses, I suppose it's all that bouncing up and down on the back of them bikes keeps 'em toned, or perhaps Ken's getting caught up in all this 'appy family bullshit and is looking at Sarah as more than a quick shag. Well if he is then he'd 'ave to clean his act up a bit coz, as fat as she is I can't see her being that interested in Ken.

The club was coming along nicely and was bang on schedule, well the main part of the club was anyway. I say the main part because what Roger decided to do was buy the land on the end and put a motel and function hall on it. I only found this out when I went down there to see how it was coming along. This was typical of Roger and exactly why I didn't trust the fucker. Don't get me wrong, I liked Roger and I know he's got plenty of time for me but he was one very dodgy geezer. Fuck knows how he got planning permission so quick! Part of me didn't wanna know, that way I could distance myself from whatever he done but curiosity got the better of me, and besides, I'm an equal partner in it so I needed to know what was going on in case the shit hit the fan and I had to cover my arse, so I arranged to meet him on site the next day.

"Jim, how you doing mate, long time no see, where you been

hiding, the lads were starting to get a bit worried about yer?"

"I'm good, things couldn't be better, in fact me and Tracy are getting married."

"So that's why you ain't been around, all loved up and ready to settle down are yer?"

"Leave it out, I ain't ready for the pipe and slippers yet."

"Glad to hear it Jim, you're far too young and stupid for that."

"I ain't that young and I ain't that fucking stupid either."

"How old are yer, twenty-five, twenty-seven?"

"Twenty-nine actually."

"Twenty fucking nine, you're still a kid and as for stupid, well, you got involved with me so you can't 'ave too much up top."

"Yer, looking round at this lot I think you could be right."

"Don't be like that Jim, what's the problem, come on talk to me, what's bothering yer?"

"Well it would've been nice if I'd been consulted 'bout going into the hotel business, I thought we were building a fucking night club."

"We are Jim and that's your baby, the hotel complex is mine, it was too good an opportunity to pass up, think about it, we're building the newest bang-up-to-date club outside the city. Punters are gonna come from all over the place, the last thing they wanna do when they've 'ad a skin full is drive home is it?"

"No you're right, they'll get a cab like they always 'ave done when we 'ad the old club."

"The old club Jim, that's right and it worked quite well, but the only similarity with the new one is the name. You see the thing is, in a town of this size you're not gonna up the numbers much more than we 'ad before and trust me, nothing's worse than a half empty club so the plan is the main building will be a cabaret club. You know the sort of thing, somewhere where you can watch a good band or comedian and at the same time 'ave a decent meal."

"You mean somewhere that caters for old fuckers, that's shit. That is, it ain't what I want."

"Hang on let me finish, the function hall as we call it will become the night club so everyone's 'appy. Think about it Jim, all ages want a good time, those old fuckers that you seem to 'ave a problem with will spend good money on the right night. They might not drink a gallon of lager like your average piss-head kid but the mark-up on grub and a room for the night ain't to be sniffed at, trust me there'll be something for everyone, a multipurpose club if you like."

"You got it all sussed out ain't yer?"

"Let's just say I know my shit Jim, I'm good, I'm the best."

"You say the night club side of it is mine but I know fuck all 'bout cabaret and catering."

"Nah nor do I but I know a man who does, his name is Den and I've sorted out a meet with him next Friday at the Ritzy, you can make that, I hope?"

"Yeah no problem, I look forward to it, I ain't 'ad a good night out for fucking ages."

"So what do yer reckon then Jim?"

"Sounds great, I just wish you'd run things by me first, that's what you do in a partnership, I was gonna 'ave my wedding do at the club, now I'll 'ave to 'ave a rethink."

"Wedding do, I don't remember you running that by me."

"I didn't."

"Exactly."

"My wedding piss-up is hardly on the scale of what you've done."

"Don't matter mate, it's still a decision you made off your own back, and the reason you did is coz you knew I wouldn't be bothered, am I right?"

"Well yeah."

"Same as I knew you wouldn't be bothered 'bout my little plans, so it appears we seem to know how each other ticks, that's good Jim."

"Ticking, yeah that's 'bout right, you're like a fucking time bomb, tick tick ticking, waiting to go off at any time, I never know what's gonna 'appen next."

"Yeah Jim you're right, I well and truly took the piss, I should of got you more involved, trouble is Jim you're a worrier and if we done it your way we'd still be running a poxy pub disco for spotty oiks. Be honest now, if I'd suggested burning the Punch Bowl down would yer?"

"No, no I wouldn't."

"I rest my case."

"You're right, I do worry, I spent eight long years inside and I worry that being connected to you I'm gonna end up back there."

"Yep, that's a very real possibility."

"Great, you could of at least tried to put my mind at rest."

"I've always been straight with yer Jim, you can get out any time yer want but you love it, so you want in."

"I'm not so sure now, the fire was one thing, I dread to think how you managed to get planning for this fucking lot, what did you do, kidnap the head of planning's kids or threaten to blow his knee caps off?"

"No, nothing like that, persuading Mr Wilkins was a doddle, you gotta know your enemies' weaknesses and strengths. We all like the good things in life – fast cars, bikes, boats, a line, a bottle of whisky, a holiday in the sun, a bet on the horses. Now Mr Wilkins had a passion for leggy blondes with big tits; unfortunately his lovely wife is a short dumpy brunette. So?"

"So you set him up and threatened to tell his missus."

"You got it in one Jim, so that's one less thing you gotta worry about, the only one who should be worried is Mr Wilkins, worried his wife never sees those photos, and as long as he continues to play ball, she never will."

"You nasty fucker."

"Nasty fucker, that's a bit harsh Jim. Now if I got my planning permission and then sent the photos anyway then yes I agree, but as it stands I gave Mr Wilkins probably the best two hours of his life, I know blokes who'd give their right bollock to shag Lucy."

"What, Lucy from the Ritzy?"

"That's the one."

"Lucky bastard!"

"And all that cost him was a signature."

"You see that's just it, I don't know you at all, I thought you was just a fucking good club manager."

"I am but I've got my fingers in a lot of pies, you don't know one half Jim."

"Well if we're gonna be working together then I think it's time I did."

"Well if you was worried before then you'll be shitting yourself by the time I've finished, you sure you wanna know?

"Yeah, go on."

"Right here we go, you've got three brothers Jack, Mike and Stan, or as they were known, the good, the bad and the ugly. Jack was the eldest, a very hard but fair bloke, when it came to a business deal or any kind of negotiation he was ruthless but he always looked after his own, loyalty means everything to him. Mike on the other hand would sell his granny for a fiver and not give a shit, Jack is hard, Mike is psychotic. I've seen him beat the shit out of someone, then for good measure pull their arms out of their sockets, he's one nasty fucker. Then you had Stan the ugly, I say had, because he's brown bread now. He had a bad accident as a kid and it left him blind in one eye and a nasty scar down his face, he was only ever happy when he was off his head on booze or drugs, it was the drugs that killed him in the end."

"Overdose did he?"

"Nah silly fucker, overdone it with the LSD and thought he could fly, he jumped off an eighth floor balcony in Benidorm. Jack was gutted, he always looked out for Stan, him being the youngest and all that. After Stan's failed attempt at flying, Jack went very anti-drugs, he hated 'em and that's where the problems started between him and Mike. Mike had just done a big deal after months of planning with some Mr Big he met in the States. Jack couldn't talk him out of it, he knew if Mike pulled it off he'd want more, the profits on one shipment were around five million quid."

"Fuck me that's one 'ell of a shipment."

"Yeah, probably the biggest shipment of cocaine this country's ever had, it cost Mike everything he had. Anyway as I was saying, Jack couldn't talk Mike out of it so he went along with it and let Mike use his yacht, the English Rose. Now as you can imagine, no fucker wanted to bring it in, so part of the deal was the Columbians who sold 'em the shit arranged the crew from their end. Now this is only speculation, but no one believes Jack wanted that shit to hit the streets, so he tipped the Old Bill off and when that boat dropped anchor off the Isle of Wight it was curtains for the drugs and the Columbians; thing is though, Mike had a bloke on the inside."

"Dickson."

"Yeah that's right, now he didn't know who tipped 'em off but it was too late to cancel the shipment so instead of the south side of the island the drop was on the west. Now Jack don't know that Mike knows about the tip off so he's stuck his number one in there to make sure it all goes to plan and likewise so has Mike. Anyway, on the night there's the Old Bill and the coast guards all round the south side while the drugs are nicely being taken ashore and hidden round the west side. Well everything was going to plan until a speedboat came flying in with a load of trigger happy coons; all hell was let loose. The upshot of it is, Mike's blokes got blown away along with the coons and half the Columbians. The other half and Jack's bloke Nick are all now spending about thirty years at Her Majesty's Pleasure and the drugs, well, half of 'em were never found and I don't suppose they'll surface for about another twenty-odd years when Nick's due out. So understandably Mike was pretty pissed off, he lost everything. Jack was alright, he'd built up a nice little property empire in London, so he gave Mike one of his clubs which turned out to be the biggest mistake of his life. Mike was a psycho alright but he weren't fucking stupid! He spotted irregularities in the books straight away and the next thing you know Jack's doing a six year stretch for laundering and tax evasion. Mike will deny it till the cows come home but Jack's convinced he grassed him up. You following so far?"

"Yer I think so, so you've got three brothers all gangsters, one tops himself coz he's ugly."

"No Jim, you're not paying attention, he tries to fly and fails."

"Whatever."

"And I wouldn't say Jack was a gangster, more a dodgy businessman, Mike on the other hand made Al Capone look like the Pope."

"I don't get it, if they were brothers why they'd grass each other up?"

"Well Mike always felt like number two and to be fair he was, he saw the drug deal as his way of stepping out of Jack's shadow. Now if Mike pulled the drug deal off, not only would he be stepping out Jack's shadow, he wouldn't need Jack anymore and that worried Jack coz, although he'd hate to admit it, he needed Mike and like I said, Jack hated drugs coz of Stan."

"Yeah I get all that, what I don't get is where the coons come in?"

"Yeah, our Jamaican friends, well it turns out the Columbians sold the same shipment twice, clever little fuckers when you think 'bout it."

"Well not really, coz two big buyers ain't gonna be buying no more are they?"

"See that's the clever bit, the Columbians were a bunch of fucking chancers who happened to come buy a very large quantity of cocaine; they weren't the big boys Mike and the Jamaicans thought they were, they're probably sitting pretty on a beach in Hono fucking lulu sipping cocktails and living the life of Riley."

"So the two brothers and the Jamaicans are all at war?"

"No Jim, Jack and Mike went their separate ways and the Jamaicans just accepted they got screwed like everyone else; the one man that can change all that is Nick and as he's got about another twenty years, no-one's too worried at the moment."

"That's a great little story but what the fuck's that gotta do with you and me?"

"You still ain't fallen in 'ave yer, yer daft fucker, what if I told yer the brothers are Mike and Jack Warren."

"Fucking hell, I was inside with Jack."

"That's right Jim, I know the story and you spent a bit of time with Nick in the Scrubs if I'm right?"

"Nick, fucking hell yeah."

"So you'd be more than happy if I told yer you're now part of Jack's firm, seeing as you saved his arse inside and all that."

"Too right."

"Well, you're part of the Warren's firm alright and I'm sorry to say it's Mike's."

"Shit, I don't get it, why would Mike want me on his firm, after all I saved his brother's life?"

"And that's why, you see the way Mike sees it is he's got one over on Jack.

"Jack thought a lot of you Jim and he tried to steer you away from all this so Mike's well and truly laughing his bollocks off now coz Jim me old son, you're in the brown stuff right up to your neck."

"You weren't wrong 'bout me shitting myself, I feel sick, what the fuck can I do?"

"Nothing, just keep your head down and as long as you stay in you'll be alright, Mike needs blokes round him he can trust and so far he's been hearing good things 'bout yer so you should be alright for now. I'll try and look out for yer best I can but I'll be honest with yer,

I know how Mike ticks and one day he'll fuck you up big time."

"Funny you should say that, Ken said the very same thing."

"What, that dirty bastard from the bike shop?"

"Ken's alright."

"Yeah, you've been spending a lot of time at his place ain't yer."

"Well as he's gonna be my brother-in-law and my best man yeah I have."

"So you get the picture Jim?"

"So I'm partners with psycho Mike, not you?"

"Partner no, you're just a very small cog in a very big machine Jim."

"And what 'bout Ray, where's he fit in?"

"You and him 'ave got a bit of history I understand?"

"No not really, I nicked his Jag back in sixty-four, I'm just curious how he went from odd job man to the big I am, club owner?"

"An odd job man, that's right, an odd job man in the Grand in sunny Brighton. Well, years ago before the days of cheap holidays to Benidorm and battles on the beaches, Brighton was one of your main holiday destinations for us Brits. Most of the hotels are run down now but the Grand is still going strong and the reason is, it was then and still is the poshest hotel there, the rich loved it. Back in the early sixties Ray had a nice little earner there."

"Nice little earner, it didn't look like that to me, it looked a shit job."

"Let me finish Jim, when I say nice little earner I don't mean the shit wage and the occasional tip, no them flash suits and shoes didn't come from some tatty little shop in Carnaby Street, they were your finest quality made to measure Saville Row. You see Ray's old man, Tony, was one of the best house breaker safe crackers there was, he got Ray the job at the Grand so he could get the names and addresses of the rich punters that were staying there.

"In some cases Ray would even go through their rooms while they were sunning themselves on the beach, get their keys, pass them on to his old man, who got copies cut and in the time it's taken them to get a nice tan, Ray's popped the keys back in the room."

"So how did Ray manage to get into the rooms at the hotel?"

"Well, our Ray's a good looking bloke ain't he?"

"Yer I suppose so, he's not my cup of tea but I know what yer mean, the girls do seem to like him."

"Well it weren't long before he was knocking off the hotel receptionist, Lucy."

"Would this be the same Lucy from the Ritzy?"

"You got it, well their little scam worked quite well."

"Hang on a minute, if Ray's old man was such a good burglar why go to all the trouble getting keys cut?"

"I don't fucking know do I, perhaps he was pissed off climbing through windows, he was getting on a bit, look stop interrupting and listen, I'm freezing my nuts off here, I wanna get home."

"Yeah go on, so the three of 'em 'ave got a nice little scam going, so how's he go from scammer to club owner?"

"It starts getting interesting now, you see Jack and Mike loved the seaside, Brighton in particular. When Jack got out back in 1970 he stayed at his favourite hotel, The Grand."

"Don't tell me Ray was still a fucking odd job man!"

"Course he fucking weren't, by this time he was managing the bar or restaurant. I don't fucking know but what I do know is they were still robbing the punters."

"And they robbed Jack?"

"That's right."

"Silly fuckers."

"Well they weren't to know were they? Jack was just another rich bastard from London. When Jack got back home he went fucking ballistic, he couldn't get his head round it, he had the best security system money could buy, his place was like Fort Knox and he needed it. His missus had a passion for one off pieces of jewellery worth thousands, Ray and his old man must of thought they hit the jackpot! Well like I say he went ballistic, he put the squeeze on every known fence in the country, he knew sooner or later he'd get it back. Well lucky for them it was later coz it gave Jack time to calm down, I tell yer if he'd got hold of 'em in that first week he would of fucking killed 'em and it wouldn't of been quick either."

"So what's he do then?"

"Well once he got 'em in and found out the extent of their little scam he was well impressed, so impressed he realised they could be very useful to him."

"So Ray and Lucy went to work in the Ritzy, what 'bout Tony?"

"That's right, when they took it over it was a shit-hole but with help from me we turned it round. Tony's talents were used to get hold of documents from council officials and MPs. With Tony on board, Jack had access to all sorts of information."

"So they didn't mind working for Jack then?"

"Ray and Lucy didn't, they loved it and still do. Tony weren't too keen but he didn't have much choice; the way Jack saw it was Tony owed him about five years, that's what he would have got if he turned him in to the Old Bill."

"So is he still working for him now?"

"Na, poor fucker snuffed it two years ago."

"Now I'm getting a bit confused and lost here. If Ray works for Jack, why the fuck has he got me tied up with you and Mike's lot?"

"Ray's alright but half the time he's coked up, he ain't got a clue what's going on behind the scenes, he didn't know anything about you and Jack. He owed me a few favours so when you come in wet behind the ears and shit loads of cash he sent me your way, I tell yer what, he's in for a right bollocking when Jack does find out."

"And what 'bout you, if you're in with Mike's firm why are you telling me all this and why you so pally with Ray?"

"Well to be honest with yer, since Jack got out he's calmed down a lot, in fact he does very little that's dodgy these days, apart from the odd back hander here and there, and that ain't enough for me. I like the buzz, I like the excitement, I like being fucking dodgy, it's what I do best, I ain't the sort of geezer that's ever gonna settle down."

"I used to say that, I don't wanna be like everyone else, but I met Tracy and it changed the way I think, perhaps that's what you need, a decent bird."

"Been there done it, it bored me fucking stupid."

"I'll ask yer again, why tell me all this and why you so pally with Ray?"

"The thing is Jim, I like you mate and I feel sorry for yer, I just think it's only right you should know the full picture and like I said I'll try and look out for yer, and as for Ray, well you know him, he's a fucking good laugh. He's a great bloke to be around, he's like a fucking fanny magnet, you ever fancy a bit on the side, hang round Ray, he's always got plenty spare."

"So he and Lucy ain't an item anymore?"

"Nah they're as bad as each other, fucking coke heads."

"So Mike ain't bothered you hang out at one of Jack's clubs then?"

"I don't suppose he knows and if he did he wouldn't give a shit; listen Jim, we all go back a long way. Jack and Mike 'ave got mutual friends and mutual enemies, it ain't like all that playground stuff (you're in his gang so I'm not talking to you); no Jim, we're all big boys now."

"So when do I get to meet Mike and his merry men?"

"On your wedding, they'll all be there, we love a good piss-up."

"They fucking won't, friends and family that's all, that's all that's gonna be there."

"That's right, friends and family, consider us all as your extended family and you won't go wrong; you distance yourself like you have done lately, that's when you're gonna end up in trouble, trust me. Jim don't look so worried mate, now you know the score, you'll be fine, you'll love it, let me put it another way, the last three months, enjoyed it 'ave yer, visiting all the family, staying in watching a load of shit on the box?"

"To be honest I've been bored shitless."

"Three months, fuck me, I don't hold out much hope for you and married life mate, what you gonna be like in three years."

"It ain't always gonna be like that, once the wedding's over I can get back to normal."

"Get back to normal, I love it, you class going up the Ritzy three times a week as normal, how many of your old mates do you reckon go clubbing it three times a week?"

"I don't really see much of 'em now but Ron and Charlie, probably once a month."

"Yeah that's right, you see Ron and Charlies' other halves don't wanna go clubbing it every week and if they don't wanna then why should they? So to keep the missus happy they just go up the local for a few pints after work; now you Jim, you've got the perfect excuse, you own and run the fucking club, how perfect's that?"

"Well they reckon they're happy with that."

"That's bollocks mate and you know it, its called making the best of a bad situation and you ain't ready for that, not for a good few years yet."

"You're probably right."

"I know I'm fucking right, now listen mate I'm gonna shoot off now, I was hoping to get a bit of fishing in before dark, catch up with yer next Friday."

"Next Friday?"

"The Ritzy, our meeting with Den."

"Yeah, yeah I'll see you there 'bout nine."

"Just one last thing. Jim, what's been said today stays between us, it goes no further and that includes Tracy and her greaseball brother, understand?"

"Yeah loud and clear, see you next Friday."

Well, I walked away from that little chat not knowing whether to be scared, excited, worried or happy. The one thing I knew I had to do was tell Tracy. I now know what I'm getting myself into, it's only fair she does too, coz if Roger's right and Mike does fuck me over she's gonna know in the long run anyway and as Judy said, honesty is the best policy. Well, I gave Tracy the slightly edited version of the conversation (I left out the bit 'bout Mike pulling arms out of sockets and the fact that Roger classes him as a psycho) and she took it quite well; as she quite rightly said, it's my life and if I'm happy with it, then so is she. Once it'd sunk in after a couple of days, I was alright, in fact it was like a kick up the arse. I needed it, I'd lost interest in the Punch Bowl – I think it's taken so long for it to reopen I forgot just how much I enjoyed it.

The meeting at the Ritzy with Den and Roger went well. It was decided that for the first six months, Den would help us out. He'd been running cabaret clubs for the last three years and he knew his stuff. In fact it weren't just running clubs, he managed bands and promoted tours and basically knew all there was to know about the music industry. He'd also worked with a lot of the top bands in the sixties before they made it big. His passion was live music, he reckoned the function hall would make a far better live venue rather than a disco and who knows, he could be right but for now I'll stick to what I know.

Well, June soon came round and Tracy was well excited about the wedding. I on the other hand was more excited about the club reopening and showing it off to my mates and family. We decided in the end that the opening night weren't gonna be for the general public, it was invitation only. There were so many friends and family and what with Mike's lot you couldn't have fitted any more in. I have to say the wedding went well. I enjoyed every minute of it which surprised me really, coz to be honest I weren't really looking forward to it.

I somehow didn't think that family, friends and gangsters all in one place would go down too well but everyone chatted and had a right laugh. The entertainment was first class, Den only went and got the Drifters in, they were fucking great, they must have cost a fortune. The old, the young the in-betweens, everyone was up dancing, they loved it. The evening really did throw up a few surprises, Ken being the biggest, he really made an effort. He'd gone on a diet at Christmas and managed to shift a few stone, he looked great in a suit and spent most of the evening with Sarah and Steven.

It was the first time he'd met Steve and seeing them together you couldn't deny Steve was his, so it looks like Sarah and Ken are an item now. Bunny and Dave ain't changed, she's still gorgeous and Dave was off his nut as usual, Ron and Charlie were well pissed, they seemed to have a great time; it was the first time I'd met their partners and I was really surprised. I imagined them to be typical fat arse mums that stayed home and baked cakes all day but they were a couple of nice looking birds. I managed to have a chat with most of me mates, the conversation with Ron and Charlie must have lasted all of ten minutes, that was enough! I feel bad saying it, them being mates and all that, but they really are a couple of boring farts. All they go on about is things we done in the past, don't get me wrong we did some pretty stupid things and we had a right laugh doing it, but that's the past, the thing is I'm still a silly fucker now and getting into all sorts of shit and I can't see that changing for the foreseeable future. I think the problem with them is they've slipped into that married rut that Roger was going on about and their lives are so fucking boring now it makes 'em feel good to talk about the good old days. The good old days, how fucking sad is that, they're only twenty-nine, fuck me I ain't ready for that shit till I'm at least seventy and even then I'll probably still be fucking around getting up to no good!

I didn't see much of Judy, I introduced her to Tracy and that was about it, they seemed to get on really well so I left 'em to it. Tony and John were there but all it was was a quick, hello mate how you doing, get stuck into the bar, it's free all night. I managed to 'ave a good chat with Dave and Bunny, they seemed to be the only ones on the same level as me. They had a right result, the old couple they lived with down in Kent got killed in a car crash and they only went and left the big old house to 'em, it was worth a fortune. Bunny wanted to sell it and buy something smaller and live off the profits but Dave weren't 'aving none of that, he knew that money wouldn't have lasted 'em five minutes.

I never knew exactly what they got up to down there, I'd heard from various different sources it was some sort of brothel or swapping club. Dave called it a club for the seriously well off who enjoyed the good things in life, the good things being cocaine and sex. Anyway, the way Dave saw it was, it gave him a good regular wedge each week so he'd be mad flogging it. We promised to keep in touch and this time I think I will; the reason I didn't when I first got released was I wanted to distance myself from anything dodgy, that's a laugh, look at me now! The one bloke I tried to avoid was Mike, I'd heard so much about him he shit the life out of me. I managed to avoid him till about half ten which was good coz I'd had a few by then; now this could have worked for or against me. You see if I'd been sober, I would have come across all weak and pathetic coz I was shit scared of him and that ain't really me. He wouldn't have met the real Jimmy so I would have been judged unfairly; normally I wouldn't give a shit if someone liked or disliked me but in this case I was rather quite hoping he would.

(Roger) "Jim, great do mate, come and meet the boss, Jim this is Mike, Mike this is Jim."

We shook hands, he nearly bust my fucking fingers, he had hands like club hammers.

"Jim, nice to meet you son, I've heard a lot about yer."

"Yeah likewise."

"What you heard then Jim?"

"I've heard you're a pillar of society, a real gentleman, an asset to this great country of ours, nah not really, I've heard you're a right hard bastard and you make Al Capone look like the Pope!"

Well Roger nearly choked on his prawn vol-au-vent but that's me, I am what I am, a cocky confident fucker as someone once called me. I ain't gonna change and besides my Dad always told me, be yourself. Not everyone's gonna like yer but the ones who do will be genuine; as it 'appens I said the right thing, I smiled and Mike laughed so the ice was well and truly broken.

"I like that Jim, any comparison to Al Capone is alright by me, Al Capone, clever bloke Jim."

"Well he weren't that clever coz they got him on tax evasion."

"That's right Jim, you know your history, silly fucking thing to get done for, we know someone else who got done for that, don't we Rodge?"

When they stopped laughing Mike said, "'ave yer seen my brother since you been out Jim?"

"No I ain't, he made it clear our paths don't cross no more."

"Ungrateful bastard ain't he?"

"Well to be fair he did see me alright."

"Yeah you spent your money wisely son, this place is a little gem."

"Yeah, we're pleased with it ain't we Rodge?"

"Jim I won't keep yer long it being yer special day and all that, I'm sure your gonna wanna get back to that lovely wife of yours, mind you your mate seems to be keeping her amused."

"Yeah that's Dave, he's harmless enough he just can't help himself, fucking perv."

"As I was saying I won't keep you long, I just want you to meet some of the lads, you've got Phil, Alex, Tony, Dave and Rob on the end."

"Alright lads."

"You'll be seeing a fair bit of them and hopefully me in the future. Jim, we like your club, now Jim listen to me if, there's anything you need sorting out or help of any kind don't hesitate, there ain't a lot we can't do."

"Is that right, I don't suppose you can sort us out a holiday at short notice, we were supposed to be going to stay at Tracy's uncle's place in Cornwall but it burnt down a couple of days ago."

"Tony, over here mate, who's at the villa at the moment?"

"Terry is, he's due back Wednesday."

"How do ya fancy a couple of weeks in the Costa Del Sol Jim?"

"Yeah terrific."

"Right, Tony's gonna sort yer flights out tomorrow, you about in the afternoon?"

"Yeah."

"Right, Tony's gonna meet you here, he'll give you all the shit you need, now you 'ave a good honeymoon, you'll love it there. Terry's gonna be with yer for a couple of days, he'll show you around but don't worry, the villa's fucking massive."

"I don't know what to say."

"How about cheers Mike."

"Cheers, I really appreciate it."

"No problem Jim, look at it as a wedding present from me and the lads, now get back to your missus, I know you said he's a mate but he's getting a little bit too friendly for my liking."

"Yeah you're right I will, catch yer later, cheers."

Once I'd managed to get Tracy away from Dave and tell her the news she was well chuffed. I didn't see but apparently Mike had a chat to her earlier and she reckoned he was a really nice bloke and I have to say so do I. He was not what I was expecting, don't get me wrong, he looked like he could handle himself but he didn't come across as psychotic and trust me I've met my fair share of psychos over the years both in the nick and out! He just came across as a genuinely nice bloke, one of the lads, there was none of this Mr Warren bollocks like there was with Jack, and the holiday in his own personal villa, what a touch that was. I couldn't wait.

The next day as promised Tony dropped by the club with all the details and Sunday night we were off to sunny Spain. We arrived there at twelve and were met at the airport by Terry. Now I don't know if Terry had the hump coz he had to pick us up, or he just took an instant dislike to me, but the thirty minute ride to the villa was fucking painful. Every time I tried to start a conversation, he'd just answer yes or no, by the time we got to the villa I'd given up. I thought I'd give him the benefit of the doubt and try again in the morning.

"Morning Tel, what's the plans for today?"

"It's Terry or Terrence, never Tel, understand."

"Start again shall I, morning Terrence what we got planned for today?"

"The only ones that call me Terrence are my Mum and Dad, so it's Terry, alright?"

"Loud and clear, so you gonna show us round are yer?"

"Since when 'ave I been a fucking tour guide?"

"Since Mike said you'd show us around I guess."

"He did did he, well you better grab some breakfast and be ready to go in about an hour's time."

Exactly one hour later Terry's out the front blaring the horn and revving the bollocks of the motor, this was one guided tour I weren't looking forward to. I got the distinct feeling Terry didn't like me too much, which I could expect if he actually knew me, but as I've only just met him it pissed me off a bit, but me being the persistent fucker I am, I gave it one last go.

"So Terry how did you know who I was at the airport, there must have been over two hundred or more coming through them gates."

"Seen you up the Punch Bowl ain't I."

"I don't remember seeing you up there, when was this then?"

"Why would yer, I was just another face in the crowd and you was pissed out your 'ead anyway, it was the week before it burnt down."

Now I haven't spent long round Terry but when he said about the

Punch Bowl burning down it was the only time I'd seen him smile. He showed us all round Malaga, we had something to eat then headed back up the hills to the villa. The villa was about a fifteen minute drive from the town; like Mike said it was fucking huge, it had its own pool and tennis court and the views were stunning, problem was me and Tracy didn't drive.

"Terry before you go, you got the number for a local taxi?"

"You ain't gonna get a taxi to come up 'ere."

"Fucking great, how we meant to get about?"

"The motor's staying."

"We don't drive."

"You're fucked then, no wait a minute there's a couple of scooters in the garage. You can handle a fucking scooter I hope?"

"Yeah no problem."

Terry went back that evening and before he went I was gonna 'ave it out with him, I wanted to know why he was such a miserable cunt and why he didn't like me. I accept that I'm not everyone's cup of tea but at least give me a fucking chance. I didn't confront him coz like I say I've met some psychos in my time and Terry was right up there with Norman Bates; when he said about the Punch Bowl fire his eyes seemed to get bigger, he looked fucking menacing. Anyway once he'd gone me and Tracy had a great time; getting round on the scooter was a bit of a laugh, it brought back a few memories I can tell yer, in fact I promised myself I'd get another one when I got back.

We got back from Spain and felt great, it was just what the doctor ordered; we were both getting stressed out with the whole Mike thing but now we'd met him and had a chance to get used to the idea, it weren't too bad. In fact it all seemed a bit exciting. Tracy was even thinking of coming to work in the club instead of the bike shop but I weren't 'aving none of it. Two reasons, really the main reason being I don't want her connected with anything dodgy and the other thing is if married life does, like everyone says, get a bit boring I can always escape down the club. I can't see it 'appening but best be safe than sorry, that's what I always say.

It's true what they say, time flies when you're having fun and the first two years did we have fun; life was one big party being part of Mike's firm, we stayed at his villa a few times and thankfully there was no psycho Terry there. It turns out it's not just me he's got a problem with, Roger reckoned the only ones he's got any time for are his Mum and Dad so we only saw him a couple of times up the club and when he was up there he'd only ever talk to Mike. Fuck knows what his speciality was but as we didn't see much of him I didn't give a shit. The rest of the crew were a good laugh; you had Tony, he was a short stocky bloke, I suppose he must have been about fortyish, they were all between forty and fifty. Tony was like the organiser, if you need tickets for flights, football matches, concerts, anything, Tony could get 'em; when one of the clubs or restaurants needed work doing to it then Tony sorted it. Then there was Alex, he was your typical office boy, in fact he reminded me of my old English teacher. Alex was the number cruncher, the firm's accountant, the most important part of the firm, he balanced the books perfectly and he needed above all to look what happened to Jack. Phil, Dave and Rob were your typical leg breakers, they were the frontline troops so to speak, each one had five or six equally hard bastards under them, I'd met a few of 'em down the club. Roger used to get 'em to work the door if ever we were short of a bit of muscle. That was more or less it, really Mike's firm consisted of about twenty-five to thirty extremely dodgy characters. I think I'd met most of 'em at some stage, all but one and I've saved the best to last and that's Vinny, Mike's son. The reason I hadn't had the pleasure of meeting him yet is he's currently serving ten years for GBH and attempted murder; you see young Vincent is one extremely nasty fucker, at the age of ten he cut his next door neighbour's dog's throat coz it kept barking. When he was fifteen he got expelled for beating the shit out of one of the hardest kids in school; he thought he'd been judged unfairly so that night he broke into the school and slaughtered all the school pets.

At eighteen he came to work for his Dad, he was part of Rob's crew; now Rob's crew were running the protection of some of north London's boozers. All Vinny was meant to do was look and learn, a sort of apprenticeship if you like but that weren't enough for him. He loved the power, he loved to see the fear in the poor fuckers' eyes they were extorting money out of. He was itching to have a go, he'd been with Rob for about three months and Rob decided to give him his chance to prove himself. It was a boozer in Willesden, the geezer who run it Sid, was ex-army, a bit of an 'ard bastard, so you can imagine how the poor fucker felt having to give over his 'ard earnt cash to a bunch of low-life scum who'd never done a 'ard days graft in their life. I mean this geezer was old school, he served his queen and country and fights by the Queensbury rules, he was a proud man so you can imagine how he felt when Vinny, who's more or less a kid, has not only asked for the two hundred but another score on top coz it's his birthday; it was too much for Sid, he flipped and told Vinny to go fuck himself. Vinny's done no more, he's jumped the bar and cut Eddy to fucking ribbons when he got out of hospital a week later apparently he looked like a patchwork quilt, he was a right mess. It was bad enough what he done but the silly fucker done it in full view of Sid's missus and about fifteen regulars, Mike tried to buy 'em off but Sid's missus weren't 'aving none of it, she wanted Vinny done and quite rightly too. He was a fucking animal; Rob's no shrinking violet but it even shocked him just how savage an attack it was. When Roger told me the story I said, father like son then, but he reckoned Vinny was a lot worse, even Mike ain't too bothered he's banged up.

This was the one thing that bothered me and Tracy; although we weren't the ones robbing, extorting and conning we were still part of it all. We still enjoyed holidays in the villa that was bought with the proceeds of Mike's protection rackets, money that had come from poor fuckers like Sid and I can tell yer it didn't sit easy with us, but like

Roger said, while we're in it we're alright, break away and who knows what's gonna 'appen so we kept our 'eads down and minded our own business.

The club had been running for four years now and fashions and trends change, the cabaret side of things weren't that great. In fact the disco was keeping it afloat so me, Roger and Den 'ad a meeting and it was decided that the cabaret club would become the night club and the night club would be a live music venue. This is what Den said all along but like Roger said, you don't know till yer give it a go and I think four years was long enough. It was decided that Roger would run the disco and Den would help me get the venue up and running. Initially I was a bit pissed off 'bout it but Den took me to the Marquee in Wardour Street and gave me a taste of what the kids were into and I have to say I loved it. The band that were giving it large and whipping the kids to a frenzy were The Jam, they reminded me of The Who, all that slashing guitars and attitude. The venue was up and running in seventy-eight and by the summer of seventy-nine the Mod revival was taking hold in a big way. It was good to see scooters buzzing round again, I couldn't resist, it I had to get another Lambretta. I know I was old enough to be some of these kids' dad but I didn't give a shit, I was eighteen again. I always felt I was robbed of my youth getting banged up, so now I was picking up where I left off. Ken took the piss a bit which was rich coming from him, seeing he's still ripping round on bikes. The kids thought I was great being an original and all that, plus the fact that the bands I was putting on at the venue were mainly Mod bands. Riding round on me scooter and looking sharp in my two tone suit was as far as I took it; when it come to aggro at the seaside I left it to the kids. In my day it was just Mods and Rockers, now you got Punk, Skinheads, Mods, Rockabillies and Greasers, of which half of them are your original Rockers, and not forgetting the Soul boys, and they all seemed to hate the Mods. It weren't just Ken who took the piss, Roger and the rest of 'em didn't take me too seriously anymore.

I think they looked at me as a bit of a joke but I didn't give a shit, I was 'aving a right laugh and the venue was making big bucks.

Well, like I say music and fashion change, and by eighty-three the Mod revival seemed to fizzle out. The venue was still making good money but my heart weren't really in it. I wanted to get back into the night club but Roger weren't 'aving none of it and he was right. From a business point of view it didn't make sense, we were both running the clubs like clockwork. I used to pop in there occasionally but I didn't feel like one of the lads anymore. In fact it got to the point where I felt about as welcome as a turd in a swimming pool. I was starting to feel like I didn't belong, and this began to worry me a bit. It got to the point where if me and Tracy fancied a night out clubbing we'd go to the Ritzy. I wanted out. I know Roger told me to stay in and I'll be alright but that was eight years ago. Surely if Mike was gonna fuck me up, he would have done it by now. Anyway, I couldn't see what he could possibly 'ave on me so I decided to sell up my side of the club, and so I got Tony to arrange a meet with Mike.

"Jim come in, what can I do for yer?"

"I want out Mike, I wanna sell up my half of the club."

"You do, do yer? Well it ain't as simple as that, anyway I thought you loved that club?"

"I do but I wanna spend more time with Tracy and the kids."

"I don't blame yer Jim, she's a lovely girl and I've got the perfect solution, how about I get you an assistant manager so you can take more time off."

"Nah I want out."

Mike leaned forward, looked me in the eye and snarled.

"No Jim you don't, my boy Vinny's out of nick next week, they're letting him out early for good behaviour and you're gonna show him the ropes son."

"You are joking, right?"

"Am I fucking laughing?"

"No."

"Vinny's no good to me on the street, he's a sick fucker, he's too over the top. I want you to look after him and keep him out of trouble. Vinny's very enthusiastic, if we can get him to channel that energy into helping you run the club instead of cutting people up then he's more use to me."

"I'll do my best."

"That's right Jim, you will."

Mike the psycho, well I hadn't seen it before but Roger was right, that five minute conversation changed everything. I was now seriously worried. I ain't no Bamber Gascoigne but it don't take a genius to work out what the future holds for me. In fact I was so worried I didn't tell Tracy; now normally I told her everything but I couldn't see how both of us being shit scared was gonna help. I had to talk to someone, Roger was definitely out, Ken was too close to Tracy, the only one I could think of was Dave. I hadn't seen him since the wedding, that was eight years ago, I just hope the coke ain't damaged too many brain cells. I know he's a bit of a prat but he ain't stupid, so I jumped on a train and headed off down to Kent. As soon as I got out the taxi Dave couldn't wait to rip the piss out of me, he started shouting.

"We are the Mods we are the Mods we are, we are, we are the Mods, Jim how you doing you nutter where's your scooter?"

"Yeah, yeah very funny, it's at home in the garage."

"Fucking hell it's true then?"

"Yeah I got a scooter, you gonna ask me in or what?"

"Come in Jim, it's good to see you mate, what can I get yer, tea, coffee, beer or something a bit stronger?"

"I'll 'ave a beer Dave."

"So what you doing still bombing round on scooters Jim, me and Bunny pissed ourselves when we found out."

"Well I just got caught up in it all didn't I, I was booking Mod bands and as you can see I don't drive so I got myself a scooter to get about on. I weren't wearing a parka and all that, leave it out Dave, it ain't that fucking funny you piss taking wanker. No bollocks, why should I make excuses and try and justify myself to you, yeah I was a Mod again and I loved it, it was fucking great! I still like the clothes, the music and yeah I still ride my scooter and why shouldn't I, Ken still rides a bike."

"Why shouldn't yer, coz it's fucking daft that's why, you own a night club for Christ's sake, you should be driving round in a Merc or a Bentley."

"I thought I owned a night club, it's all gone wrong Dave."

"What do yer mean, you either own it or you don't?"

Well, I told Dave more or less the whole story.

"Hang on a minute let me get this straight, you gave this Roger geezer who you'd only known five minutes, a half share of the club?"

"I didn't just give it to him did I, it was on the condition he got the place extended and doubled the profits."

"Well he did, didn't he?"

"How was I to know he was gonna burn the fucking place down?"

"So Roger was just fronting it for Mike?"

"Yeah that's right, and what worries me is when Mike's psycho son gets the hang of running the club."

"You'll be surplus to his requirements, I'd be worried too, you're a daft fucker Jim. I said to Bunny at your wedding you were in way above your 'ead. Some of them geezers you were talking to are big time dealers, I know Jim, I've dealt with 'em."

"I know all that now don't I, what do yer reckon I should do?"

"Start praying mate."

"Come on I'm serious."

"You ain't got too many options 'ave yer. If it was me I'd cut my losses and just walk away, you must still 'ave a few quid stashed?"

"Yeah I 'ave but he ain't 'aving none of it, he wants me there helping psycho Vinny."

"Emigrate."

"Tracy will never do it, she's too close to her family."

"Grass em up, go to the old bill, you must 'ave shit loads on 'em?"

"Who's being fucking daft now?"

"The way I see it you've got no choice, show Vinny the ropes get to know him, become his new best friend. If he's a sick fucker, he ain't gonna 'ave too many mates is he, so his old man is probably gonna be well chuffed if you and Vinny get on."

"Yeah you're right, trouble is I fucking hate him already, it ain't gonna be easy pretending to like someone you don't."

"It's a doddle Jim, I've been doing it for years, how long 'ave I known yer?"

"Yeah I do wonder sometimes, anyway that's enough 'bout me, I wanna know what you and Bunny get up to down 'ere, I've been straight with you so no bullshit."

"Right, it doesn't go no further, if Bunny knows I told yer she'll do her nut."

"Where is she anyway?"

"She's at her Mum's for a few days, her old man snuffed it last week."

"Go on then spill the beans, you're into all that swapping ain't yer you dirty bastard!"

"No we ain't, so if yer give us a chance I'll tell yer. I think it was seventy or seventy-one, me and Bunny went to Spain for a couple of weeks, the hotel we was staying in was a right shit-hole, in the middle of nowhere. We'd only been there a few days and we met Derek and Cynthia at this little restaurant, they were getting on a bit."

"How old were they?"

"Late forties early fifties but they kept 'emselves looking good, she had a lovely arse, anyway they were a right laugh so we went out with 'em a few times, it was obvious what they wanted."

"What was that then?"

"They wanted to shag us didn't they?"

"And you did didn't yer, you dirty git."

"Hang on I was getting to that, so anyway they were staying in this villa, they asked us if we wanted to stay with 'em, Bunny was well up for it."

"She ain't shy is she?"

"She didn't wanna shag 'em you prat, she just wanted to get out the hotel, you should of seen it Jim, it was falling apart. I had a few too many one night, I've leaned on the sink to chuck up and the fucking thing came off the wall. Bunny 'ad enough so we packed our gear and went up to their villa. The first couple of nights we just chilled, out played cards and got pissed. They weren't shy, our room overlooked the pool, when we went to bed they'd have a late night swim with fuck all on. Anyway on the last night we went to our favourite restaurant with 'em and when we got back to the villa Derek asked us if we wanted to do a few lines of coke. Now me and Bunny are up for most things, we'd done uppers, downers, smoked dope, a bit of LSD, we even tried magic fucking mushrooms but we hadn't done coke, probably coz it was too expensive. Anyway we thought, fuck it we'll give it a go, Jim it was fucking great, I've never felt so horny."

"So you ended up shagging 'em."

"All night mate, she was a fucking animal, she took it up the arse and everything, at one point I was shagging 'er and…."

"Alright, alright spare me the gory details, I get the picture, didn't it bother yer that Derek was banging Bunny's brains out in the next room?"

"I weren't exactly thinking of Bunny at the time was I. In the morning when the drugs 'ad worn off we're all sitting there with our orange juice and boiled eggs and I started to get the 'ump a bit. Bunny and Derek kept smiling at each other, then I started to imagine them together."

"I bet you wanted to kill him?"

"No I got a hard on actually."

"Fucking 'ell Dave, you ain't normal."

"That's rich coming from the oldest mod in town."

"Me being a mod is 'ardly comparable to you getting turned on by some geezer shagging yer missus."

"Let's talk 'bout normal shall we, neither one of us are what your average boring Mr and Mrs 2.5 kids would class normal are we, let's be honest. We just get our kicks in different ways, you choose to act like a teenager and 'ang round gangsters, I choose to 'ave a varied and exciting sex life, you tell me Jim what do you class as a normal sex life?"

"I don't know do I, I know one thing, it ain't what you and Bunny get up to that's for sure!!"

"Alright then you tell me what sex is, what do you actually get from sex?"

"Leave it out Dave, can we drop the subject, you and Bunny are a couple of dirty fuckers, each to their own, good luck to yer."

"No bollocks, I gave you a chance to defend yourself and yeah, I did think you were a prat for riding round on yer scooter but now I see where you're coming from and I have to say it sounds a bit of a laugh, so now your gonna 'ear me out."

By this time we were well pissed and Dave was starting to get out his pram a bit so I humoured him and let him 'ave his say.

"What is sex and what do yer get out of it, well it's a bloke and a bird touching each other's bits and getting turned on, it's physical ain't it and when you come it feels great."

"So how often do you and Tracy shag?"

"Enough."

"How long you been together?"

"'Bout eleven years now."

"I bet you're down to once or twice a week?"

"Yeah 'bout that."

"Why's that then Jim, bit fat and ugly now is she, not ageing very well?"

"No she bloody well ain't, she's as gorgeous now as she's ever been."

"So why you gone from wanting to shag her brains out at every opportunity to only once or twice a week then?"

"Coz that's what 'appens when you get married."

"Yeah that's right but why, right shut your eyes, dig deep into that tiny brain of yours, go back to when you first met Tracy. You there?"

"Yeah I'm there."

"Right, did you think, she's a nice girl I'd like to take her home to meet Mum and one day marry her, or did you think, fucking 'ell she's a bit of alright I'd love to give her one?"

"You know the answer to that?"

"Yeah course I do, it's the same thing that goes through all our 'eads when we see a bird we fancy, its natural ain't it?"

"Your point is?"

"Hold up I ain't finished yet, right close your eyes, now go back to the first time you was alone and starting to get intimate, you'd dreamed and fantasised about that moment for weeks and there you are about to fulfil all your dirtiest fantasies, remember the buzz, the anticipation, the excitement as you put your hand up her skirt and slipped your fingers up the leg of her knickers, remember how good it felt watching her face as she come for the first time?"

"Alright Dave, yer I remember, it was fucking great."

"Well is it right that you're never gonna experience something as fantastic as that again, you're gonna deprive yourself of something that gave you so much pleasure."

"Yeah I see what you're saying but I enjoy being married more."

"Yeah I agree but why can't yer 'ave both?"

"Coz Tracy would fucking kill me that's why."

"I ain't just talking 'bout you, I mean both of yer, why should she miss out?"

"So what you're trying to say is you and Bunny are into all that wife swapping?"

"No, we're not."

"You've just told me you swapped with Derek and his Missus."

"Yeah we did, coz we fancied 'em."

"What's the fucking difference?"

"Look mate, the last time me and Bunny shagged anyone was probably about four years ago, we don't just shag for the sake of it, there's got to be something there, some sort of chemistry."

"Yeah well, that's the danger, coz that chemistry is love ain't it?"

"Course it fucking ain't, it's sexual chemistry, once you've shagged each other's brains out you get dressed and fuck off home. You don't want a repeat performance coz it's that buzz you get off on, it's the build up, it's a bit like a kid with a Christmas present, they see it under the tree for weeks, the excitement builds, they can't wait for Christmas day so they can rip the paper off and see what's inside, once they've unwrapped it and played with it for a few hours they get bored with it, you see the fun's in the unwrapping."

"Yeah I see what yer saying, but it ain't for me, you can't 'ave a very good marriage if that's what you're up to."

"It's the opposite mate, we've got a fucking good marriage, in fact all the couples that use our club 'ave been married for like twenty, thirty years. You see, to do what we do you've gotta be one hundred and ten percent secure; if there's any weakness or insecurities in the marriage then fucking around with other couples will end it, and I have to say Jim, me and Bunny are more solid and happy now than we've ever been."

"That's good Dave, I'm glad to 'ear it, so that's what you do then, run a swapping club?"

"No, that's how we started, when we first moved 'ere we done a bit of everything, I looked after the grounds and Bunny cleaned and looked after the house and in the evenings we looked after the clients. When Derek and Cynthia snuffed it we changed it all, now we arrange high class hookers for very wealthy clients and we do a bit of dealing."

"You fucking idiot."

"Yeah you're probably right, but what's life if you ain't got a bit of excitement in it."

We ended up drinking well into the morning, we were well pissed and the more pissed he got the more he let on what him and Bunny got up to. I was actually starting to get a bit jealous, there have been a few occasions when I've been tempted to shag someone else but I ain't coz I wouldn't want to lose Tracy. All that shagging other people lark sounded alright, that was until he let on that the couple they last swapped with was Charlie and his Missus! I was well shocked, they seemed so normal and boring, anyway it didn't work for them coz they ended up getting divorced. They took the chance, whereas I ain't prepared to risk what I've got, anyway it ain't right is it, some other geezer shagging your Missus.

Once I'd sobered up I headed back home. Dave might be a right crude fucker but like I say he ain't stupid and what he said 'bout being Vinny's best friend made sense, I didn't wanna but it was my only option. Vinny was released the following Thursday, Mike rang me personally and asked me to be at the club for eight, I didn't have much choice. Trust me the last thing I wanted to do on my night off was celebrate the release of a psycho, anyway I got down the club for about seven-thirty. I was expecting welcome home banners and the whole of Mike's band of merry men but instead there were just the normal regulars. Mike turned up bang on eight with Vinny. My first impression was he looked your typical hard case, short hair, tall, well built and he had the trade-mark club hammer hands like his dad and uncle.

"Jim this is Vinny, Vinny meet your new boss!"

"Alright Jim pleased to meet yer."

"Right I'll leave you two to get to know each other."

"So Vinny you wanna help run the venue do yer?"

"No not really but I gotta do something I suppose."

"So has your old man told yer much 'bout the venue and me?"

"Nah not really, he just said you put bands on and that, and he reckons we should get on coz we're pretty similar."

"Similar, he's 'aving a laugh, how's he work that one out?!"

"He reckons you've done a good job of running this place but you're a bit of a prat."

"A prat, why's that then?"

"He reckons you're always pissed and you still ride round on a fucking scooter."

"And that makes me a prat does it?"

"Well yeah it does, listen Jim I don't know why you're getting so upset, I'm his fucking son and he's put me on the same level as you, how do yer think I feel?"

"I don't get it, you were released today?"

"Yeah that's right, what don't you get?

"I don't get why you're sitting 'ere 'aving a beer with me, why ain't you out celebrating with your mates, why ain't yer dad and the rest of 'em 'ere, I don't get it?"

"I ain't got no mates and I don't want fuck all to do with the firm, between me and you, I ain't got a lot of time for the old man either. It's coz of him I've just spent ten years inside."

"Is that right, is it, so he put the knife in yer hand and forced yer to cut that poor fucker up did he?"

"You don't like me do yer?"

"Well let's just say I don't like what you've done, I don't know yer yet, so I can't say."

"I like you Jim, I like yer a lot."

" 'ang on a minute, you don't bat for the other side do yer coz I'm 'appily married?"

"No I fucking don't, in fact I ain't got a lot of time for geezers full stop."

"So what's it 'bout me then?"

"You're right when yer say you don't know me, you've probably 'eard 'bout Vinny the psycho and all that shit I've done in the past. I ain't gonna try and defend myself coz it was pure evil but I've 'ad a lot of counselling inside and I'm a lot better now. That's why they let me out early, I know why I done that shit and I'm learning to deal with it."

"You ain't gonna tell me you've found God are yer?"

"Am I bollocks, I ain't into all that shit."

"Go on then, why did yer then?"

"Well it turned out it's all to do with my childhood."

"Bullied were yer?"

"Yeah I was."

"Fucking 'ell I would never of 'ad you down as a kid that got bullied, I thought your sort were born 'ard."

"I weren't bullied by other kids you knob, I was the 'ardest kid in the school, nah, it was my old man, he used to beat the shit out of me, you see I was the youngest, I've got four older sisters."

"Most dads would be chuffed to 'ave a boy after four girls."

"Yeah and my Dad probably would of as well, trouble is my Mum died 'aving me and from what I've been told my old man fucking worshipped 'er, so I guess that's why he's never 'ad any time for me."

"So he brought you up on his own."

"Nah, course he didn't, he didn't 'ave any time for me at all, my sisters did. Anyway this counsellor reckoned I was always trying to impress my Dad, trying to do things I thought he'd like. I wanted him to not only be proud of me, but to actually like me. You must of 'eard the one 'bout me killing the next door neighbour's dog."

"Yeah."

"Well I actually liked dogs but I knew it was pissing the old man off keep barking all the time so when he said he'll fucking kill it one day, I done it for him. That's why I blame him for ending up inside. I thought if I could be this super 'ard gangster he'd be proud of me. Anyway, after spending so long inside I realised I don't actually 'ave much time for blokes, I was only really 'appy when I used to go out with my sisters and their mates."

"Yeah, I can see why you've got a problem with blokes, coz of your nasty bastard Dad, so why do yer like me?"

"Well the one bloke who actually cared 'bout me was my uncle Jack and you saved his life."

"Yeah that's right and it cost me five years, so if yer don't want anything to do with yer Dad's firm why you 'ere?"

"What else am I gonna do with my record?"

"You could always get a job in an abattoir."

"Very funny, anyway there can't be a lot dodgy 'bout running a poxy club."

"No there's not, who knows you might even like it, I love it."

Vinny turned out to be alright, I suppose I had a bit in common with him; when I was growing up I always felt like my sister was always the favourite. My old man weren't nowhere near as bad as his but he used to knock me about a bit, mainly when he was pissed. The other thing we 'ad in common was Jack, neither one of us see him now. Vinny was alright as long as I kept him away from any aggro. I made the mistake of putting him on the door one night, never again! It was a Saturday night, most of the crowd were in and there was these three geezers hanging around the door, Vinny asked 'em to come in a couple of times and they just ignored him so he said to 'em,

"You either pay your money or fuck off."

With that the biggest one took a swing at him, Vinny went berserk. I ain't seen nothing like it, he beat the shit out of all three of 'em and I mean beat the shit out of 'em, two were taken away in an ambulance. Lucky enough we 'ad a few witnesses to back him up or he would have gone down again.

For the next three years me and Vinny worked together well, we became good mates. Mike left us alone but just as I was starting to feel secure and safe again Vinny hit me with a bit of news that was gonna change everything.

"Jim you've gotta go, you've gotta walk away from all this."

"What the fuck you talking 'bout?"

"My old man he wants you out, he reckons he don't need yer no more."

"You're winding me up."

"No straight up, I'm serious, I was round there last night. I don't know what he's got on yer but he reckons you'll be going down for a good few years."

"He ain't got fuck all on me."

"He might not but trust me one way or the other he wants you out, look Jim this 'as got fuck all to do with me, you know that don't yer?"

"Yeah, yeah."

"I tried to change his mind but he weren't 'aving none of it, he wants you out by the end of the week. Jim I'm gutted, you've been like a brother to me, you're the only one that's given me a chance, I hate him, I wanna fucking kill him."

"Look Vinny don't worry 'bout it, I've always known I was on borrowed time, I'm amazed he's waited this long."

"What you gonna do?"

"Let me get this straight, if I walk that's it, end of story, he'll leave me alone?"

"Yeah."

"Well fuck it, why wait, I'm off."

"Jim wait up, we're still mates ain't we?"

"Yeah we're mates, you're alright Vinny, don't worry, I'll see yer around."

Well I can't say I was too surprised. I was gutted though, all the time, money and effort I put into that club and it's gone just like that. Mike shafting me weren't no big surprise but what 'appened a week later knocked me for six. I was walking down the road to get some fags and this Merc pulled up alongside me, the window went down and this big geezer said,

"Jump in, Mr Warren would like a word."

Now my Mum always told me never talk to strange men and certainly never get in their cars and besides I was shitting myself so I told him, "Tell Mr Warren to use the fucking phone like everyone else."

"Just get in you cocky fucker."

Well I got in, the way I see it was, he'll get hold of me sooner or later and anyway this geezer didn't look the patient type.

"So who are you then, I ain't seen yer before?"

"Why should yer?"

"Well I've seen most of Mike's firm up the club or venue at some stage, don't recall seeing you."

"I said Mr Warren not Mike, why don't yer fucking listen."

"You mean Jack?"

"I mean Mr Warren."

"Mr Warren, what's he want?"

"How do I fucking know? I'm just the driver."

"Well where we going?"

"London, The Ritzy."

"Why there?"

"I'm just the…"

"I know, just the fucking driver."

It took 'bout an hour to get to The Ritzy, I gave up trying to talk to the driver, he was like a fucking robot. I walked in The Ritzy and there's Jack sitting on his own.

"Jim, over 'ere mate, sit down, what can Andy get yer?"

"I'll 'ave a lager, cheers."

"A lager for Jim and I'll 'ave a tea, it's too early for me."

Andy brought the drinks over then left us alone.

"It's been a long time since I last saw you Jack."

"Nineteen years Jim, and in that time you ain't done a lot of growing up 'ave yer, you've been a bit of a prat ain't yer?"

"No not really, I've got married, I own a bike shop, I built up a successful club."

"That you've now lost."

"That's right, your fucking brother has well and truly stitched me up."

"No Jim, not yet but he will – you don't just walk away from Mike, he'll keep yer on the back burner for now till he finds a use for yer."

"What the fuck 'ave I done to him, why's he got it in for me?"

"You saved my arse Jim and Mike won't forget that, and lucky for you nor will I. I'm gonna make sure you're alright, but the only way I can do that is if you come on board with us."

"Yeah great, what doing?"

"You tell me, what do yer wanna do?"

"Run this place."

"Done."

"What 'bout Ray?"

"What 'bout him?"

"Well he's been running this place for 'bout eighteen years, you can't just kick him out."

"I can and I've already done it. I knew you'd want this place, you spend most of your time 'ere."

"Nah can't do it, Ray loves this place."

"That's what I like 'bout you Jim, loyalty, you even show loyalty to the geezer that helped stitch yer up."

"Yeah I suppose you're right."

"Listen Jim, Ray's history whether you're 'ere or not, him and Lucy were warned, no drugs."

"Yeah he liked his Charlie."

"I didn't give a shit what he was sticking up his hooter, I didn't want that shit being sold or distributed anywhere near me or my business."

"And Ray was."

"That's right and it was shit he was getting from Mike's lot."

"Oh dear."

"Yeah it's a fucking big, oh dear!"

"I was told the story 'bout yer brothers and the big shoot-out on the south coast."

"You was, was yer, then you'll know my best mate Nick is still banged up as a result of it."

"I never knew he was your best mate. I was told he was your top bloke."

"Anyway that's history and so is Ray."

"So if I'm in with you Mike's gonna back off?"

"Let's just say I've got plenty on him so you should be alright."

"Great, when can I start?"

"Now, Stewart will be 'ere in about an hour, he'll show yer round."

"I won't let yer down Jack."

"I know yer won't, you was doing alright with the Punch Bowl, it was a nice little boozer, it's a shame you weren't 'appy with that."

"How was I to know Roger was what he was?"

"Clever bloke Roger, I like him."

"So I've got a free hand with this place, I can do what I want?"

"Within reason, yeah."

"Great, roll on Friday."

"Right, like I say Stewart will look after yer, I'm shooting off now, you won't be seeing too much of me 'ere, I can't stand all that fucking jungle jive, be good Jim and enjoy."

"Yeah cheers."

I couldn't believe it, I ended up with what I wanted all along and

I'm going back now to when I was sitting in that cell in the Scrubs. Not only am I part of Mr Warren's firm, I'm running one of the top clubs in London! Alright it's a bit of a fucker losing the Punch Bowl but I've still got the bike shop and a fucking good screw from The Ritzy. I was well chuffed.

Word soon got out I was running The Ritzy. Vinny popped in occasionally, he was genuinely gutted when Mike kicked me out. Dave got down there at least once a month, he was doing really well and the big surprise was Charlie and Ron, they got up there every Friday. I suppose now Charlie's divorced and Ron's as good as, they've decided to live a bit. John and Tony got up there occasionally and one night Jeff turned up and I ain't seen him since Brighton '64. It was fucking great, I gradually changed the music a bit, most of the crowd that got up there were, let's just say not kids, it was a real party atmosphere. I dropped all the shirt and tie bollocks and made it more casual. I had four good years there, I couldn't do no wrong, it was fucking great. Unfortunately everyone around me was falling apart. 1990 will undoubtedly go down as the worst fucking year ever.

It started with Dave, he turned up at the club just after Christmas in a right state.

"Jim can I 'ave a word out back, I'm in the shit big time."

"Yeah course, 'ang on let's grab a few pints. So what's up Dave, someone got the 'ump with yer for shagging his missus?"

"No, it's fucking serious Jim."

"Go on then what you bin up to?"

"Well you know I done a bit of dealing."

"Yeah."

"Remember Rudy."

"Rudy, course I do, he's dead now ain't he?"

"I wish he was, silly black fucker."

"What, he's still around?"

"Yeah, he's still around, I don't know for how much longer

though, if I don't sort this shit out we're both fucking dead."

"Dave what the fuck 'ave you got into?"

"Right, I'm buying on a regular basis from Rudy, he's getting fucking good gear, the best, I'm then selling it on and doubling my money. Everything's going well, most of our clients we send girls to are major coke heads, some of 'em are worth millions. Well we got this bird, Daniella, she's fucking gorgeous, I mean she's model material mate, we send her to the big money men. Well, she's bin seeing this geezer for 'bout a year now, he's fucking loaded, he spends about fifty grand a month on girls and coke."

"Fifty grand, you're fucking joking?"

"Half of that's coke, he loves it. Well, he'd decided to sail round the fucking world ain't he and he wants shit loads of Charlie to take with him. When I say shit loads I mean seven hundred grand's worth."

"Fucking 'ell."

"Jim, I stood to make half a million profit on that little deal."

"And it's all gone wrong."

"Wrong, it's a fucking disaster, Rudy's only gone and ripped some Paddy off for about a grand. So this Paddy's followed him, waited for him to get the gear, I've met Rudy in the same place I always do and next minute I know this Irish cunt's pulled a shooter on us and took the fucking lot!"

"So, Rudy's lost a few drugs and you've lost your rich fucker's money, so what?"

"So fucking what, Jim they ain't Rudy's drugs, he's just the man on the street, Rudy's boss gave me two weeks to either come up with the drugs or the money."

"What about Rudy?"

"He's fucking legged it ain't he, that's not all, it gets a lot worse. Well I weren't getting the drugs back so I had to find seven hundred grand. I tried borrowing it on the house but because of the recession the house value's gone right down so out of desperation, I've torched it ain't I for the insurance."

"Dave that takes fucking ages to come through."

"Yeah, I know, so I've now gotta keep my 'ead down till it does. Jim, I need some cash and somewhere to stay till it comes through."

"Cashwise I can't help yer but I 'ave got somewhere you can stay."

"Nice one Jim, where?"

"Above the bike shop there's a flat and a dirty great office, it ain't being used at the moment, it's yours for as long as you want it."

"Cheers Jim."

Well, Dave was the start of it. A few weeks later I get chatting to Charlie and Ron and the poor fuckers 'ave gone bankrupt and are looking at me to help 'em out. I can't coz like everyone else, the recession has affected the bike shop, so I'm basically living off my wages from the Ritzy. Well there's me thinking I'm a lucky fucker, I'm doing alright, and I was. Well I thought I was but that was until I've gone through the accounts for the bike shop and realised we owe money left right and centre including seventy grand in VAT! I've gone into panic mode and gone flying down the shop to sort it out.

"Eddy, 'ave early lunch mate, I need a chat with Ken and Tracy, right you two what month is it?"

(Ken) "April."

"That's right and Trace, what do I do every April?"

"You've done the books and noticed."

"Noticed that we aint bin selling too many bikes or noticed we owe seventy fucking grand to the tax man."

"Jim that's down to me, Tracy had nothing to do with it."

"'Ang on a minute, am I missing something 'ere coz the last I knew, you was a mechanic, not a fucking bookkeeper."

(Tracy) "Its bin so quiet 'ere lately I've spent a lot of time next door in the salon, Deb's bin training me up."

"You sell bikes, you don't fuck around with birds' hair."

"I don't wanna sell poxy bikes any more."

"So you've left Ken to cope with it all?"

"I've bin doing alright Jim."

"Alright, we owe seventy fucking grand, what the fuck 'ave you done with it?"

"I'll pay it back."

"Ken, what 'ave you done with it?"

"Well I owed big Steve twenty grand and he was starting to get a bit heavy."

"Yeah, so what 'bout the other fifty?"

"That went on Scarlet Lady, a dead cert at the 2.15 at Epsom."

"You put fifty grand on a fucking horse, please tell me you're winding me up?"

"Do you realise how much I would've got if it'd won?"

"Ken, it obviously didn't so why am I fucking bothered, how could you be so fucking stupid?"

"This 'orse 'as bin winning everything and I 'eard a whisper from a very reliable source that it couldn't lose this race, it 'ad a bit of 'elp if you know what I mean?"

"Steroids."

"Yeah."

"So what went wrong?"

"It keeled over and 'ad a 'eart attack at the second 'urdle didn't it, the silly fucker who injected it overdosed it."

"I don't know whether to laugh or cry, if you weren't so fucking 'ard I'd beat the shit outta yer."

"Best 'ave a laugh then."

"Ken we're gonna lose this place if I don't find that money, it's called fucking bankruptcy and in case you hadn't noticed its 'appening all around, Ron and Charlie 'ave lost everything."

"What you talking 'bout find the money, you're fucking loaded, you ain't telling me you've done all that cash you got from your half of the Punch Bowl?"

"There was no cash, I walked away from it."

"What yer talking 'bout walked away, you ploughed thousands into that."

(Tracy) "Yeah Jim, what's going on?"

(Ken) "They fucked you over didn't they, I knew it, you wouldn't listen would yer and you've got the front to call me fucking stupid! How much did you lose one, two, three, four hundred grand?"

(Jim) "Difference is Ken, it was my fucking money to lose."

(Tracy) "'aving a go at each other ain't gonna sort it out, let's just go home, sleep on it and try and sort it out tomorrow, and Jim, I wanna know what's bin going on?"

Well I told 'em the full story and it didn't matter how much we went over it, the bottom line was we were fucked! We 'ad till the end of August to find the cash or the bike shop was gone.

What a bunch of losers, you've got Bunny and Dave in hiding and Rudy on the run coz a bunch of nasty bastard coons are after 'em. Ron and Charlie are doing a bit of cabbying coz they went bankrupt and it looks a dead cert we're gonna lose the shop. Just when I thought it couldn't get any worse, it was a Tuesday night the second week of August, I'm indoors watching the box with Tracy and Vinny came round. He looked like he'd won the pools but forgot to post the coupon.

"Alright Vin, what's the matter mate?"

"It's the old man, he wants to see yer."

"Nah bollocks, tell him to fuck off and leave me alone.

"Jim, you really need to see him, Jack ain't gonna get you out of this one and he wants to see yer now."

"What's it all about Vin?"

"I ain't got a clue but he wants to see both of us."

"You must 'ave some idea?"

"Trust me Jim I know fuck all, I 'aven't seen him for nearly a year and that suits me coz he's treated me like shit."

"He really don't like yer does he?"

"No he doesn't, I thought if I done a good job with the club it might change but he's still the same, I fucking hate him."

We went round to Mike's place and he was there on his own.

"Come in lads sit down relax, what can I get yer?"

(Jim) "I'll 'ave a tea."

(Mike) "Tea, what's that all about, you on the wagon or something?"

"No, I just got the feeling I'll need a clear 'ead."

"What about you Vinny, you'll 'ave a beer with your old man?"

"Yeah I'll 'ave one."

"Good, while you're over there do Jim his tea."

"Get to the point Mike, you never invited me round 'ere for tea and biscuits, what do yer want from me?"

"Straight to the point, I like that Jim, Jim tell me, 'ave you ever heard the little story about my drugs that went missing on the Isle of Wight?"

"Yeah, I 'eard."

"Then you'll know the only one who knows the whereabouts of them drugs is Nick."

"Yeah and he's inside."

"That's right, well Nick's been a good boy and we know what 'appens when you're a good boy inside don't we Vinny?"

"Yeah they let you out a bit early."

"That's right son, well lucky for me in Nick's case five years early."

(Jim) "So why's that lucky for you, he ain't gonna get your drugs back?"

As soon as I shut my big gob I realised I'd overstepped the mark. I've never seen anyone go from placid to psycho as quick as Mike. He leaned forward, the veins on the side of his head looked like they were gonna burst, his eyes bulged, I thought his fucking 'ead was gonna spin round like that kid on the exorcist, he was fucking scary! His face was about eighteen inches from mine, I was about to witness the psycho Mike I'd 'eard so much about.

"Listen 'ere you skinny streak of piss, one more wise-crack like that I'll rip your fucking arm off and beat the shit out of yer with the soggy end, you're fucking nothing you got that?"

"Yeah loud and clear."

"Well fucking say it then you cunt."

"I'm nothing."

"That's right and don't ever forget it."

By now to say I was shitting myself was an understatement, I don't think I've ever felt so fucking scared in my life; once he'd blown a gasket he went back to placid Mike.

"Where was I?"

"You were telling us about Nick coming out."

"That's right and Nick's gonna get my gear back."

"I don't mean to be disrespectful Mike, and perhaps I didn't put my point across too well but I don't think Nick is gonna be too co-operative when it comes to them drugs."

"You taking the piss Jim?"

"No definitely not, but you see where I'm coming from can't yer? He's just done twenty-five years coz of that shit, he ain't likely to risk going back for another twenty is he?"

"Yer I see where you coming from, now see if you can see where I'm coming from, 'ave you any idea what that shit's worth?"

"A few million."

"Countries 'ave gone to war for less than what that shit's worth, do yer do a bit of gear Jim?"

"No don't touch the shit."

"What 'bout you son?"

"Nah I stick to my beer."

"Well at the moment there's a serious cocaine drought, the Yanks 'ave closed down seventy percent of Columbia's drug trade. Now that shit is Columbia's finest, we're talking a street value around ten to thirty million.

"Fucking 'ell."

"Yeah fucking 'ell Jim, Nick's gonna get my shit back make no mistake 'bout that, you wanna know the best bit?"

"Go on."

"Well, as you and Nick got on so well inside you're gonna 'elp him."

"Why, I don't get it, your blokes are more than capable of bringing it in, like you say I'm nothing, I'm just a poxy nightclub manager."

"That's right, that's why you're the perfect man for the job, my blokes ain't gonna be able to shit without the Old Bill knowing 'bout it and that goes for Nick as well. So this is what's gonna 'appen, Nick's gonna tell yer where the shit is and you're gonna get it."

"I ain't doing it, I'm looking at a ten year stretch if I get caught."

"That's right Jim, what's the going rate for murder these days, ten, fifteen or is it life?"

"Murder, what yer talking 'bout?"

"I'm talking 'bout the night you killed that poor fireman at the Punch Bowl."

"That's bollocks I 'ad nothing to do with that."

"Is that right, well Terry has just signed a statement claiming you paid him ten grand to torch it."

"Why would he do that, he's gonna go down as well?"

"That's right but you see he's not too bothered, Terry unfortunately isn't very well, let's just say we won't be getting him a Christmas card this year. By the time the case comes up he'll be pushing up the daisies and you my friend will end up spending a good few years back in the nick."

(Vinny) "That ain't right."

"Shut it son."

"And if I do get yer gear what 'appens then?"

"To show my appreciation I'll pay your little debt to the tax man."

"And that's it, we're quits?"

"If that's what you want Jim, yeah."

"I ain't got a lot of choice 'ave I?"

"No Jim you ain't."

(Vinny) "So why am I 'ere?"

"You and Jim are good mates I understand, so Vinny, you're gonna give him a hand, a bit of back-up, he might need a bit of muscle."

(Vinny) "And what's in it for me?"

"Son, you've never bin any use to me, you've always bin a fucking liability. I'll tell yer what, you and Jim pull this off, the club's yours, how 'bout that? I'm cutting yer loose, there ain't gonna be no love lost between us is there, let's be honest?"

"I'm 'appy with that, you've got yourself a deal."

"Right, we all know where we stand, you've got till the end of September to sort it out. Nick will be in touch soon."

Well after that little talk with Mike, losing the shop all of a sudden became unimportant. I now stood to lose another ten years of my life coz there ain't a way in this world me and Vinny are gonna pull that one off. I mean you don't just nip over to the Isle of Wight in a dirty great van, load it with thirty million worth of gear, pop back and live 'appy ever after do yer? The only way I could see myself ending up a free man was to go to the Old Bill, tell 'em the whole story and then spend the rest of my life in hiding, and I didn't fancy that. So I decided to bluff Mike out, I rang him up and told him bollocks I ain't doing it. I couldn't see how a dying bloke's statement was enough to send me down for something I didn't do. Within two hours of me putting the phone down there was a knock on the door, I've opened it and there's Dickson and this young copper standing there.

"Can we come in Jim, I think we need a little chat?"

"Yer come in."

"This is Phil, my son."

"I would like to say pleased to meet yer but I'm not, so can we just get on with it."

"Jim I've got a warrant 'ere to search this place and arrest you in connection with the arson and murder of a fireman at the Punch Bowl in seventy-three."

"Do it then, all you got on me is a statement from a dying man."

"Yes I 'ave and quite a good one, it ties up perfectly with Rogers, times, dates, places, they're all in there and along with the ten wraps of Charlie Phil's just found in your khasi you could be looking at fifteen, maybe twenty years."

"You bastard."

"Yep a real dirty one, I'll let Mike know you'll be ringing him shortly shall I?"

"How do you sleep at night?"

"Quite well actually, I always find a nice cup of Ovaltine 'elps, you should try it although I think in your case you might need something a little bit stronger for a good while yet."

"Get the fuck out of my 'ouse you smug cunt."

"You've got precisely twenty minutes to make that call, now you enjoy the rest of the day, see you around Jim."

Twenty minutes, I made it in five, there was nothing I could do, if I 'ad all the time in the World it wouldn't have made any difference, Mike 'ad me exactly where he wanted me. The only one who might be able to get me out the shit was Jack, so I arranged a meet the next day. I told Jack everything and he just sat there and listened, then when I finished he just moved his head from side to side, he didn't 'ave to say it, I knew exactly what he was thinking, he was thinking what a fucking idiot I was.

"Well Jim I can't say I'm very 'appy 'bout all this, there's only so many times you can call a favour in and I think I've well and truly evened it out with you."

"I know and I've appreciated everything you've done but I'm

desperate."

"Jim I can tell yer now you're going down mate, the only reason Nick's getting out early is coz he's done a deal. The Old Bill 'ave been after Mike for years and Nick's gonna hand him to 'em on a silver platter along with anyone else connected to that shit. The only glimmer of hope you've got is, if you can give 'em anything else?"

"If Nick's done a deal, how come Dickson don't know?"

"Dickson's small time, he's not even a middle rung of the ladder, the top brass 'ave always suspected Dickson is bent but they've never been able to prove it."

"What if I give 'em Dickson?"

"Yeah you're going in the right direction, right shut up a minute I need to think."

Jack sat there, eyes shut, rocking backwards and forwards in his chair for about ten minutes.

"Jim I'm gonna 'elp yer one last time, when it's over all ties with me will be cut."

"What about the Ritzy?"

"It's over mate, I don't even want you in there as a paying punter, do yer understand?"

"Yeah I understand."

"Nick's getting out coz I arranged it."

"Friends in high places, a bit like when you got me that cushy kitchen job inside."

"No Jim, the governor of the Scrubs ain't quite on the same level as the Police Commissioner at Scotland Yard."

"Fucking 'ell, he's dodgy."

"No, straight as a die Charles is."

"I don't get it, if he ain't bent, where's the connection with you?"

"I'm a grass Jim and in return let's just say the rules get bent slightly in my favour, I can't work miracles but in your case I might be able to 'elp you out."

"A grass, I don't get it."

"It's simple really, you know the story 'bout my brother Stan."

"Yeah, the one who thought he could fly like Superman."

"Find it funny do yer Jim?"

"No, no I don't it's fucking sad really."

"The thing is Jim, when my Mum was on her last legs, I promised 'er I'd look out for Stan, it was bad enough losing Stan but I felt I let my poor Mum down."

"Yeah I can see why you don't like drugs."

"I don't like the maggots that deal in 'em Jim and if I in some way I can get 'em off the streets I think my old Mum would be proud of me."

"So you grassing up drug dealers is a sort of therapy for yer?"

"That's right Jim, I like that, therapy I suppose it is in a way, anyway I'm gonna arrange for you to 'ave a little chat with Charles, to see if he can help you out."

I was meeting Charles the next day in London, I 'ad all night to come up with something else I could give him, hoping it'd be enough to keep me out of nick. I had shit loads on Mike and his dodgy dealings but they were gonna get him anyway. I hit a blank, I couldn't think of anything. It was about eight and there was a knock on the door, it was Dave, he popped round to see if I fancied a beer. As soon as I saw him at the door, it came to me.

"Jim do yer fancy a few beers mate, it's doing my 'ead in sitting in that flat all night?"

"No mate, I've got shit loads of paperwork I've gotta sort out but come in, I've got a few cold ones in the fridge. Dave, these dealers that are after yer, big time are they?"

"They don't come much bigger, I'd say fifty percent of the gear in London's supplied by them."

"So how long they been supplying then?"

"How long, well how long we known Rudy?"

"Since about sixty-three."

"Well there you go, nearly thirty years."

"So them Blues we were popping like Smarties came from these geezers that are after yer now."

"Well where did yer think Rudy got 'em."

"So Rudy's small time then?"

"Rudy's the man on the street, there's hundreds of Rudys, he gets his gear from the big boys, cuts it up a bit then knocks it out."

"What do yer mean cuts it up?"

"Well, they add a bit of this, a bit of that to make it go a bit further."

"Like what?"

"Talc, anything that looks like Charlie."

"So you ain't got a clue what you're shoving up your 'ooter."

"Rudy's shit was good gear."

"So these geezers, the ones that are after you and Rudy they don't fuck around."

"They're Jamaicans Jim, they like their guns, make no mistake, we're fucking dead if we don't come up with that money soon."

"So if there was a way of getting them off your back for good would you and Rudy be up for it?"

"You mean grass 'em, you'd never get away with it."

"What if there was a cast iron guarantee?"

"Well yeah, I'd be quids in when the insurance for my place comes through. Jim, what's going through that tiny peanut of yours?"

"I don't know myself yet."

That was it, I had my something else to give to Charles, I didn't know at this stage how I was gonna tie it all up but at least I 'ad something to give him.

The next day I had my meeting with Charles. I couldn't tell him anything he didn't already know 'bout Mike but when I mentioned the Jamaicans his eyes lit up.

"Our trigger happy friends from the Caribbean, now that really would be the icing on the cake, you any idea how long we've been after that lot?"

"No idea, I know nothing 'bout Jamaican drug dealers, only that they like their guns."

"We were aware of the Jamaican connection back in sixty-three, back then it was just a bit of wacky backy and pills, they tried moving up a league back then but…"

"I know the story, so technically that shit on the Isle of Wight is as much theirs as it is Mike's?"

"Well not personally, the guys that are involved now, the original five that funded the deal back then got blown away along with four Columbians and four of Mike's blokes and a couple of good coppers."

"So they're gonna be more than interested in that shit then?"

"That's right Jim. Right Jim, let me tell you how this works: you tell us everything, times, places, names, numbers, the lot, you're the only one that gets the 'get out of jail free card', everyone else is going down. This is probably gonna be the biggest operation of its kind this country's ever seen. Nick will be in contact with you shortly. Once he's told you the location of the drugs it's all down to you; if this goes wrong you'll spend the rest of your days behind bars, that I can promise you, do you understand that?"

"Loud and clear, you want the drugs, you want Mike's lot and you want the Jamaicans and providing you get all that, I walk?"

Nothing like a bit of pressure, not only 'ave I gotta find a way of setting up two of the biggest drug networks in the country I've gotta find a way of doing it so Vinny don't go down, and in a way that it don't look like I've blatantly set everyone up. I 'ad my in with Mike's lot, that weren't a problem. The Jamaicans on the other hand, the only way I was gonna get to them was through Dave, so Dave had to know everything, I didn't 'ave no choice.

I didn't want Tracy knowing so I went down to Dave's flat. When

I got there Bunny and Dave were in the middle of packing their bags.

"Going anywhere nice?"

"Canada, Bunny's got relations out there."

"I don't get it, why?"

"The insurance company ain't paying out so we're getting as far away as possible, when those fucking coons find out we ain't getting their money we're dead mate."

"Hold up, hold up, stick the kettle on Bunny, you ain't going nowhere."

(Bunny) "We are Jim, the flights are booked."

(Dave) "The cab's picking us up in a couple of hours."

"So you reckon you're gonna live 'appily ever after in Canada, what yer gonna do over there anyway?"

"Bunny's uncle's got a garage, I'll sell cars."

"And you think your little dispute with the coons is gonna go away, well let me tell yer it won't, you're gonna spend the rest of your days looking over yer shoulder. If those coons are anything like the bunch of cunts I got mixed up with, trust me sooner or later they'll 'ave yer."

(Bunny) "Is that right Jim, well what do yer suggest we do?"

"Sit down, 'ave a cuppa tea and listen, I've got a way of getting 'em all off our backs."

(Dave) "Well we've got a couple of hours to kill, go on, what's your master plan?"

By the time I'd finished the full unedited version of the story the taxi was out front bibbing the horn.

(Bunny) "Great story Jim but we're off."

(Dave) "'Ang on a minute Bunny, so what you're saying is we've gotta find a way of setting up the coons and Mike's lot plus get one over on the Old Bill as well?"

"That's about it yeah."

(Bunny) "You're fucking mad, you'll never in a million years pul it off."

"What 'bout it Dave, I never 'ad you down as an Arthur fucking Daley."

"No, nor did I, I'm probably gonna regret this but Bunny, we don't need the cab, what we need are a few beers, it's gonna be a long night. Jim, 'ave you got any idea what thirty million quids' worth of gear looks like?"

"Ain't got a clue, what will we need, a big car or van?"

"You'll need a fucking lorry for that lot."

"We don't need it all do we, it don't make any difference if it's one, two, three or thirty millions' worth, the consequences are the same ain't they?"

"And what 'appens when you turn up at Mike's place with only a fraction of the gear?"

"We'll just 'ave to make sure we're not there."

(Bunny) "I wanna know how you're gonna get away with it with the Old Bill, it's alright for you Jim but what 'bout Dave and anyone else you rope into it?"

(Jim) "The way I see it is you're only gonna get done if you're caught with it actually on yer."

(Dave) "Yeah and it will be."

(Jim) "That's right but if we can somehow lose the Old Bill, deliver the gear then get out of there, we're in the clear."

(Dave) "And how we gonna manage that, from the minute your arse gets off that ferry you're not gonna be able to 'ave a shit without the Old Bill knowing 'bout it."

"Yeah Mike said the same."

Well we sat there till gone twelve racking our brains, trying to work out a way of pulling it off, then at 'bout one, just as we were gonna give up and accept the fact that Dave was gonna sell dodgy motors on the other side of the World and I was gonna do ten years, I don't know where it came from but I came up with a brilliant idea.

"Scooters, we bring the shit back on scooters."

"I think we should call it a night, you've ad one too many Jim."

"They are never gonna know it's us, trust me."

"What yer talking 'bout, two middle-aged geezers riding scooters with shit loads of cocaine on the back, notice us, you daft fucker, we'll stick out like bulldogs' bollocks."

"Yeah you're right, but what if there was 'bout three thousand middle-aged geezers on scooters."

(Bunny) "I'm going to bed, he's pissed."

"No wait up listen. August Bank Holiday is scooter weekend on the Isle of Wight, it's the biggest scooter rally of the year, you're probably looking at about ten thousand scooters."

"So you're saying we're gonna ride over one hundred miles on scooters, load up the gear and back again, you ain't gonna get fuck all on two scooters are yer?"

"On two no, but what if there was about six of us."

"Yeah there'd be enough."

"Right this is what we do, we get a big removal truck, you know one of them big fuckers with a ramp on the back, we load up six scooters at the bike shop, we get on the island, load up enough gear that can be carried on six scooters, then on the Monday when most of 'em are coming home we drop the back down, ride out and lose ourselves."

"Two problems with that, one, there's only two of us, who's the other four, and second, you 'ad to be straight with that copper Charles."

"Right, there's me and you, Vinny, Ken, Charlie and Ron."

"Me you and Vinny, no problem we've got nothing to lose, how you gonna convince the others?"

"Ken owes me big time, he ain't gonna be a problem and Charlie and Ron, well they ain't exactly got glowing futures in front of 'em 'ave they?"

"Yeah but it's a better future then at least ten years behind bars."

"We do this right none of us are gonna get caught and we all walk away with a nice lump sum."

"And where's this lump sum coming from?"

"You must still 'ave your contacts, I'm sure a couple of packs of that shit ain't gonna be missed, what 'bout the geezer who was gonna go round the world?"

"Yeah, he's got so much money he just looked at that dough he lost as an inconvenience, if this shit's pure uncut Columbia's best like you say it is, all we'd need is the amount it takes to fill a spare wheel on a scooter; and what about the copper, what yer gonna tell him?"

"We tell him we're bringing it over on scooters and a lorry."

"He's gonna want to know why we're splitting the load?"

(Bunny) "Why are yer splitting the load?"

"Right, we take our lot on the scooters to an arranged drop with Mike, we drop it then get out of there, as soon as we're out we tip the Old Bill off, the lorry goes to an arranged drop with the coons."

"Who drives the lorry then?"

(Jim) "Rudy."

(Dave) "So Rudy goes down with the rest of 'em?"

"Yeah."

"I don't know if I'm too 'appy 'bout that Jim."

(Bunny) "What you on about not 'appy, it's because of that idiot we're in the situation we're in now, if anyone's going down I'd rather it be him than us."

(Jim) "Yeah Dave, you ain't got no loyalties to him, and from what Ron and Charlie 'ave told me he was a nasty fucker at one point."

(Dave) "That was fucking years ago, Rudy's alright now, but you've got a point, rather him than us!"

(Jim) "Right you've gotta find Rudy, and make sure the word gets out to his boss, I'll 'ave a word with the others and let's meet back 'ere on Saturday and go over everything, what do yer reckon?"

"I reckon it's so fucking stupid it's gonna work."

Me and Dave spent the next couple of days fine tuning the plan, ferry crossings, accommodation, meeting points, times, it had to be spot on.

Convincing Ken wasn't that 'ard, like me and Dave he didn't 'ave too much to lose, things weren't that great between him and my sister and it looked like we were gonna lose the bike shop so he was well up for it. The only thing that bothered him was 'aving to ride a scooter. The only way I could convince Ron and Charlie was by offering 'em fifty grand and they had immunity from prosecution, so they just see it that they were gonna 'ave a bit of fun riding a scooter back from the Isle of Wight and getting paid shit loads of money.

Dave told Rudy only what he needed to know, as far as Rudy was concerned it was a straight split fifty/fifty, we were taking ours back by scooter and he 'ad the lorry. The biggest gamble I took was telling Vinny the whole story. I trusted him, and when I told him he thought it was great. I think deep down he didn't think for a minute his old man was gonna give him that club. By the Sunday before the bank holiday weekend everything was sorted, all we needed was a final meet to go over everything, just to make sure we all knew what we were doing.

"Right lads, we all comfortable, everyone got a beer, good then I'll begin. Right, the bottom line is, me and Dave 'ave got ourselves in a right load of aggro, Dave with Jamaican drug dealers and me with Vinny's old man Mike. If this all goes tits up then Dave's gonna end up dead and I'm going inside for life. It's a long story but basically we've done a deal with the Old Bill and as long as they get the drugs, the Jamaicans and Mike's lot, we're in the clear."

(Charlie) "'ang on a minute, fucking gangsters and Jamaican drug dealers, you said it was straightforward riding scooters from the Isle of Wight with a few bags of drugs, dumping 'em off somewhere in South London and that's it."

(Jim) "Yeah that's right."

(Ken) "So not only are we transporting the gear, we're setting the coons and Mike's lot up?"

(Dave) "No you're not, you don't need to know about that, that's down to me and Jim, all you've gotta do is ride the scooters and that's that."

(Ron) "I wanna know, them fuckers don't mess about, they'll blow your fucking brains out."

(Charlie) "Yeah so do I."

(Ken) "I don't give a toss 'bout the coons, how we setting the other lot up?"

(Dave) "Right, the coons are down to me and Rudy."

(Charlie) "Rudy, I thought he was dead?"

(Dave) "Unfortunately for me he's alive and kicking, it's coz of him I'm in this shit, the drugs are being split, Rudy's taking the bulk of 'em in the lorry."

(Ron) "Lorry, I thought we were using scooters."

(Jim) "Right, hold up, let us explain what's gonna 'appen, then we can do the question and answer bit. Right, I'll start again, now just listen for fuck's sake or we'll be 'ere all night."

(Ken) "We're listening."

(Jim) "Dave, you explain."

(Dave) "Right, me, Jim and Rudy are taking the lorry with the scooters on, we're getting the early ferry from Portsmouth Friday morning, the rest of yer are booked on for Saturday morning, you'll all be going in Vinny's motor. When you get there you head for the Sandbanks Holiday Park which is just outside Shanklin, we've got two big caravans there. By the time you get there we'll have the drugs on the lorry. Ken, we'll need you to give us a hand loading the gear onto the scooters. By Saturday night the lorry and scooters will be ready to go, we then park it up, go out, get pissed and enjoy the weekend, then Monday morning the fun begins. Rudy's gonna drive the lorry with us in the back to about three miles from the ferry terminal, then at about ten-thirty he drops the back down, we ride out and join the hundreds of scooterists that are all heading home. When we get to Portsmouth, we head off to a factory unit in Lewisham, unload the gear and fuck off home. Meanwhile, Rudy's heading to my old place in Kent where his brothers will be waiting along with the Old Bill. Then there'll be a massive shoot out and hopefully our Jamaican friends will get well and truly blown away. Jim's told the Old Bill and Mike's lot that the drugs will be delivered Tuesday so when they turn up we'll be long gone, all the bad guys get nicked and we live 'appily ever after, right, any questions?"

(Ken) "So why you grassing yer old man up Vinny?"

(Vinny) "Coz I fucking hate him."

(Ken) "Fair enough."

(Ron) "Why we using scooters, why don't we just load the motor up?"

(Jim) "Coz I don't trust the Old Bill, if they do go back on their word they can only do yer if they find the gear on us and they ain't in a million years gonna pick us out amongst all them scooters."

(Charlie) "Where's the fifty grand coming from?"

(Jim) "Dave's got the insurance money from his house through, by the time he's sorted you lot out he's still three hundred grand in."

(Vinny) "What if the coons get away?"

(Dave) "They won't, I've told Rudy that Mike's blokes are gonna turn up dressed as coppers so when the Old Bill turn up all hell's gonna be let loose, you know how they like their guns."

(Ken) "These caravans, who's sharing with who?"

(Dave) "Does it matter?"

(Ken) "Yer it does, I ain't sharing with no fucking coon."

(Jim) "You'll be with Ron and Charlie."

(Ken) "That's alright then."

(Ron) "Sounds like it's gonna be a bit of a laugh."

(Ken) "Yeah I can't wait, riding a scooter, how exciting, if my mates see me I ain't gonna 'ear the last of it, they'll be taking the piss forever."

(Jim) "That's a point, Ken, you ain't gonna be able to wear your usual clobber, you're gonna need a parka, come to think of it you're all gonna need to get some gear to wear. We've gotta fit in with the rest of em, we all need a little trip to Carnaby Street to get kitted out. Right, we've got time, tomorrow we all meet back 'ere at eleven, we need to go shopping, are there any more questions before we go, is everyone 'appy, right, see you all tomorrow?"

It took a while, but we got there in the end, everyone seemed 'appy enough, the only one who weren't was me. I weren't 'appy about putting Ken, Charlie and Ron at risk; if it all went tits up then not only would I be going down but they'd be going with me and that didn't sit well with me. I went over the plan a thousand times, I couldn't see how they could get caught. Dave's a clever bloke and he was about ninety percent sure as well. Anyway, no-one had a gun to their heads, they knew there was a small risk, so fuck it. The next day I thought I'd get to the flat early so I could go over the plans with Dave yet again. I got there at about nine-thirty; as I was going up the steps a really gorgeous blonde passed me and jumped in a cab. I knocked on the door and Dave opened it about six inches.

"Jim you're early, can you give us an hour, I'm busy?"

"Busy, doing what?"

"Nothing, just pop back in an hour or so."

"No, bollocks, just open the door."

Dave opened the door and sitting in the corner was a lovely looking girl, a real stunner.

"Jim, this is Daniella."

"Alright love how you doing?"

"I'm doing fine."

"Dave, can I 'ave a word?"

"Yeah go on."

"No, in private."

"Yeah course, come through to the kitchen, I'll do us some breakfast."

"Dave, who the fuck is Daniella and who was the blonde I passed on the stairs?"

"Daniella's the girl I told yer about, you know the one with the rich coke head punter who we're gonna sell the gear to."

"And what about Blondie?"

"That's Susy her mate."

"And what the fuck they doing 'ere?"

"They just popped round to see me and Bunny."

"So its nine-thirty and they just popped round looking like that, bullshit."

"Alright Jim, I'll be straight with yer, me and Bunny 'ave been running a bit of business from 'ere."

"And what business is that then?"

"Well, you know we arranged girls for rich punters?"

"Yeah."

"Well it ain't just rich geezers that fancy a bit of fun is it, we all like a bit of fun don't we?"

"Dave just get to the point."

"Well we put an ad in the local paper for visiting massage and the response was fucking amazing, we charge a oner an hour."

"Dave, please tell me you ain't turned this place into some sort of knocking shop?"

"Course I ain't. I told yer it's a visiting massage, the girls just chill out 'ere while they're waiting for a job."

"I ain't 'appy 'bout this Dave, we'll sort it out when we've dealt with all this other shit."

Well, by the time I'd had my little chat with Dave about his new business, the rest of the lads were there so we shot off to London to do a bit of shopping. It turned out we had a bit of a laugh, we bought a load of gear from Carnaby Street then had a little look round Leicester Square and Soho, even Ken enjoyed it!

By Monday night everything was sorted. All Ken needed to do was pick the lorry up on Wednesday and make sure the scooters were checked over and ready to go. I thought, great, I've got three days to relax; well, that was until the phone rang Tuesday morning. It was Judy, she'd left her husband Bob and was at Heathrow airport with three suitcases and nowhere to go, that's all I fucking needed. I hadn't even told Tracy I was off to the Isle of Wight with her brother and the lads, and now I've got Judy turning up in an hour or so. Tracy thought it was great, she really liked Judy and before I could tell her I was off with the lads for the weekend she suggested we all go out clubbing on Saturday.

"I can't love, I was gonna tell yer today, me and the lads are off on a scooter weekend to the Isle of Wight."

"When was this arranged then?"

"Yesterday when we was up London."

"Who's going?"

"Me, Dave, Ron, Charlie, Vinny and Ken."

"Ken, what you on about, he can't stand scooters and Mods."

"Yeah I know but he's been on a bit of a downer lately and he thought it might be a bit of a laugh."

"Yeah you're right, I'll 'ave a word with Bunny and Sarah and we can all 'ave a bit of a laugh."

"No leave it out Trace, it's just me and the lads, anyway you won't get booked in anywhere now."

"Why won't we, you did yesterday, right, cut the crap, what's going on, you're lying and you ain't going anywhere till you're straight with me."

I told her the whole story, and rather than put her off, she was more adamant she was going.

"I can't believe this could be the last weekend we spend together and you weren't gonna tell me was yer, you was just gonna go?"

"It ain't gonna be the last weekend, the reason I didn't tell yer is, I knew you'd wanna go and it's just too risky."

"If you're so sure it ain't gonna go wrong, why's it so risky then?"

"Alright go."

"I am, does Bunny know?"

"Yeah."

"What about Sarah?"

"Course she don't and she don't need to either, alright?

"I'm saying nothing, you stay here and wait for Judy, I'm going round to see Bunny and Sarah."

She'd only been gone ten minutes and Judy arrived.

"'Ello gorgeous, let's stick yer bags in the other room and I'll put the kettle on, you must be gasping."

"Yeah, cheers Jim I am."

"So what's been 'appening with you and Bob, Trace said you've left him?"

"That's the problem, nothing's been going on, that's why I left him, he don't wanna go anywhere or do anything, he'd turned into a right boring old fart, I can't remember the last time I had a decent shag."

"Bloody 'ell, as bad as that is it?"

"I've given him plenty of warnings but he's took no notice, I've had enough, I'm too young to give it all up, I want a bit of fun, a bit of excitement. I don't think I've kept in bad shape 'ave I?"

"No, I was about to say you look fucking good, in fact you've got better with age."

"Ahh Jim, you're so sweet."

"I must admit when I came to see you that time, I was surprised you'd got into all that dope smoking hippie shit, you was always the life and soul of the party."

"Yeah, you and me had some fun didn't we, it's a shame you was so into that slapper Bunny, are her and Dave still together?"

"Yeah they're still together alright, in fact Tracy's at their place now trying to sort out the weekend."

"What's happening the weekend then?"

"Well it was meant to be a lads only thing, we're all going to the

Isle of Wight, there's a big scooter rally."

"You're joking, you lot still into all that?"

"I am, the others ain't, they're just going for the crack."

"Yeah it sounds like a bit of a laugh."

"Well if Tracy's sorted you out somewhere to stay then it looks like you, Bunny, Sarah and her are going."

"Great, that's just what I need."

Tracy got back from Bunny's, she was well chuffed; she got booked up alright, not only did she get booked up but she managed to get accommodation on the same site as us, I couldn't believe it. Now normally I wouldn't give a shit but this weekend was far from normal. It could go any way but the one thing I knew for sure, it was gonna be a fucking good laugh. By Wednesday night everything was sorted out. Now the girls were going it was decided that me, Dave and Rudy would still go in the lorry but the others would all go down together. I was 'appy 'bout everything and pretty confident, the only thing I weren't too 'appy about was Rudy. I'd heard different things about him, some good, some bad. Dave reckoned he was well sound so I trusted his judgment, after all Dave's neck was on the line the same as mine. The last time I saw Rudy was down the café when I bought shit loads of Blues off him and that was over twenty-five years ago. I got down the bike shop Thursday afternoon at about four, me and Ken loaded the scooters up and all the bags. I was just about to walk out the door and who should walk in but Rudy. I couldn't believe it, he stood there and it was like I'd gone back to sixty-four; he didn't look any different, he still had the same pork pie hat on that he used to hide his bag of pills under.

"Rudy, fuck me you don't look no different."

"Jim it's been a long time, you still one fucked up crazy mother fucker!"

"I suppose I must be, I'm about to go on a weekend break with you."

"Yeah it sounds like we're gonna 'ave some fun Jim."

"Yeah it'll be fun alright, look I've gotta shoot off, Dave's upstairs."

"Where you going man, we've got a lot of catching up to do?"

"I know and we've got a three hour journey in that thing tomorrow to do it, I'll catch yer later."

I would love to have had a chat with Rudy, but it didn't seem right getting all pally and talking 'bout the old days like he's some sort of long lost friend. I mean in three days he was either gonna get his brains blown out or end up getting nicked and it was all down to me and Dave setting him up. Besides, I had to get back coz I was meeting Nick at my place so he could fill me in on where the poxy drugs were. When I spoke to Nick earlier he told me he didn't want Tracy or anyone else for that matter there, so Tracy went out with Judy and Bunny.

Nick got to mine at eight as promised. "Come in Nick, it's been a long time."

"Twenty odd years."

"Nah, not as long as that but it's been a while, I'd like to say it's good to see yer."

"Trust me, the feeling's mutual, what a fucking mess you've got yourself into."

"It ain't that bad, I think I've got it all sorted, I just need to know where the gear is?"

"So do I Jim."

"Nick, what the fuck do you mean?"

"Well I know roughly where it is."

"I thought you were the one who hid it?"

"Yeah, that's what everyone thought, the truth of the matter is Jim, everyone got screwed on that fucking deal, no one trusted anyone, everyone was out to line their own pockets, the only one who weren't was Jack and he basically wanted to fuck everyone up."

"What, including you?"

"No it was the other way round."

"I don't get it."

"What don't you get?"

"The whole fucking lot, Roger hasn't told me the full story has he?"

"He don't know the full fucking story, stick the kettle on, make yourself comfortable, it's gonna take a while."

"Nick, with all due respect I don't wanna know, I just wanna know where the fucking gear is?"

"Trust me, you need to know."

"I'm listening."

"Right, you know the story about Stan."

"Yeah."

"Well as you know, Jack went completely anti drugs, he wouldn't even take a fucking aspirin; the thing is, we could all see that drugs was where the big money was. Back then Mike and Jack were equal, all profits were split, Jack invested his in property while Mike spunked his up on birds and fast living. Jack never stashed cash, as soon as he had enough for another pub, flat, house or business he'd buy it whereas Mike, he got off on the whole flash git thing. Mike was always trying to be number one."

"Yeah I know all that, Mike put all his cash into buying the drugs and Jack grassed him and it all went tits up."

"No Jim, it was me who went to the Old Bill, the whole operation was planned by me, I'd had enough of leg breaking, corruption, bank jobs and all that shit; the risks were high but the rewards were fuck all and the ones who were getting the cream of it was that fucking animal Mike and smart arse Jack."

"I thought you were close to Jack, his number one?"

"That's what I wanted him to believe, you see I'm the clever fucker 'ere not Jack. I knew if I could someway create a little war between them they'd either kill each other or they'd end up inside."

"Well you ain't that fucking clever coz Jack only got six years and

Mike's still about and you ended up doing twenty-five."

"We're jumping ahead 'ere, let's get back to the drugs, I knew there was no way you could stick that amount of drugs on a boat and just drop it off. I knew we were all gonna get done so I did a deal with the Old Bill."

"So you grassed 'em?"

"That's right, I told the Old Bill the drugs were being unloaded in a little bay on the south of the island, when all along I had a perfect spot on the west. I knew Mike had Dickson on the inside so I knew Mike would know about it."

"Why didn't Mike just postpone the drop?"

"He couldn't, that shit was on the way so I suggested the new drop site which is where I needed it to be all along. When the bulk of the drugs were unloaded it was mine and my mate Steve's job to stash 'em so they were safe.

"Well we'd stashed a fair bit and everything was going to plan then out of nowhere the fucking coons come steaming in, all guns blazing. Anyway before we knew it there was Old Bill everywhere, along with the coons, the Columbians and Mike's lot; three coppers got blown away as well, and one of 'em was the copper I'd done the deal with."

"That was a fucker."

"Yer, that's how I ended up doing twenty-five years, if them coons hadn't of turned up I would've got away with it."

"I don't get it, got away with what?"

"There were so many cases of that shit Steve took at least twelve cases of it and hid it. It was our little pension fund so to speak."

"And that's the shit we've gotta find."

"That's right."

"Well why don't you just ask Steve?"

"This is where it all gets a bit scary, you see me and Steve grew up on the Isle of Wight, we knew that island like the back of our hand, we had to hide that stuff where no one would ever go."

"Yeah, I was wondering where you keep that amount of gear hidden for so long, I mean it ain't something you can just stuff under your mattress is it?"

"What you on about under the mattress?"

"It's where I used to hide my pills."

"We ain't talking about a bag of fucking Smarties 'ere, each bag of that shit weighed about thirty to forty pounds. Anyway, as I was saying we had to hide the gear where no-one would go. Well we had the perfect place, in fact it was that fucking scary not even me and Steve wanted to go there. Jim, as a kid when you were making a fucking racket with your brothers and sisters, did your Mum or Dad ever say it's like bleedin' bedlam in 'ere."

"Yeah."

"Do you know what they meant by bedlam?"

"Yeah, it used to be a nut home in the old days didn't it?"

"That's right, people used to pay to see 'em for a laugh; well, it weren't just the poor that had the odd nutter in the family, the rich did as well. Anyway the poor nutters ended up in Bedlam and the rich nutters ended up in Oak Dene House on the Isle of Wight. Now in the old days no one liked to admit they had a fucking nutter in the family."

"They still don't."

"That's right, so they packed 'em off to Oak Dene thinking they were doing 'em a favour when in fact it was the closest thing to hell there was. At least with Bedlam the public could actually see the nutters at most times, so if they were getting tortured everyone would know, whereas Oak Dene, no one went there, not even the relatives, they were just put there and forgotten about. Well, all sorts of abuse went on there, the place was run by an evil priest called Father Morley. Well, Father Morley had all these tunnels and passageways dug under the house. It was like a fucking maze, there were rooms all under the house and this is where he used to torture the patients."

"And he done this all on his own?"

"No they were all at it, the priest thing was just a cover, they were all into witchcraft, devil worship and all that sort of shit."

"How far back we going then?"

"About three hundred years, well not many patients ever came out, they even had their own graveyard there. This place is fucking huge; well one day a bloke escaped and told everyone about it so all the islanders went up there and rescued the patients."

"What did they do with Father Morley?"

"Well in them days, if they thought you was a witch then they burnt yer alive, so that's what 'appened to all the women, and they hung the men, all except Father Morley. He got away and went down the tunnels, they couldn't find him anywhere so they bricked the entrance up and that was the end of him. No one went up there, everyone said it was haunted, people had actually seen the ghost of Father Morley, so many had seen it they went up there and searched the house coz they thought he might still be alive.

The house stayed empty for years, then one night three kids went up there to play and only one kid came running out, he said Father Morley had caught his friends so the villagers all went up to the house to look for 'em. As they approached the house, Father Morley was on the roof holding the two kids' heads, he'd killed 'em and cut their heads off. They stormed the house but couldn't find him anywhere, just the bodies of the kids. So they burnt it down and the ghost was never seen again. Well it stayed like that till just after the First World War then a millionaire Yank bought it and restored it, he lived there with his wife and two kids. They were only there about four months and all sorts of weird shit 'appened. The woman wanted to move out but the husband weren't 'aving none of it, he loved the house. After a year she'd had enough, she was gonna take the kids and leave but before she could, he killed her and his kids then jumped off the roof and killed himself. All the locals believe it was the spirit of Father Morley possessed him and made him do it."

"It just sounds to me he had enough, he didn't want to be on his own so rather than lose his family he took 'em all with him."

"Yeah it 'appens Jim, usually when it does the bloke shoots 'em or poisons 'em or they get smothered in their sleep, but how many times 'ave you heard that the bloke cuts his kids' heads off?"

"Fucking 'ell."

"Yeah spooky hey?"

"You're gonna tell me them drugs are in that fucking house ain't yer?"

"No it gets better than that Jim, you see Steve's old man was fascinated with that old house, he delved into the history of it from when it was built. He actually believed the spirit of Father Morley is still there but he didn't believe it was the spirit of Father Morley that killed them first two kids. He believed Father Morley never died and it was him holding them heads on that roof, it weren't no spirit. So Father Morley had to have had another way out them tunnels. He spent years looking, then one day he found it, the entrance was in a family tomb in the graveyard. You know, them big old stone things where the whole family end up."

"Yeah I know."

"Well he told Steve and the next day he was gonna tell the local museum. Well, that night he was driving along the coast road, a road he'd driven down a hundred times, and for some reason he smashed through the barrier and ended up dead at the bottom of the cliff. There was no skid mark or nothing, no one knows what 'appened. Well Steve was gutted, he never went anywhere near that house or that tomb but he told me all about it. Anyway, ten years after that, this yacht full of cocaine is heading to the Isle of Wight so it weren't hard for me to get involved in the planning coz I knew the island like the back of my hand."

"So you and Steve stashed the drugs in that tomb."

"No, I didn't go anywhere near it, it gave me the shits, all that voodoo shit."

"Why did Steve, after what 'appened to his old man?"

"He didn't want to, but with the possibility of making a few million he took the chance."

"So what 'appened to Steve?"

"No one knows, when he drove off with the last cases of gear that was the last I saw of him and no-one's seen him since."

"Well it's obvious, he fucked off with your drugs."

"No, no way, you see Steve was no gangster, he wouldn't of had a clue what to do with it, that's why I used him, them drugs are in that tomb or one of those torture chambers under the house."

"Well how am I supposed to find 'em?"

"I can tell you exactly where this tomb is but I ain't going within a mile of that place, it's fucking cursed."

"Bollocks to that, nor am I."

"You've got no choice Jim, from what I've been told, if you don't give the Old Bill Mike, the coons and the drugs, you're fucked anyway. I don't give a shit, all I've gotta do is tell Mike or you where they are, I'm a free man Jim."

"You better tell us where it is then. Do you honestly believe that place is cursed?"

"I don't know Jim, all I'm saying is anyone who's had anything to do with that house and them drugs has been fucked up in some way. I've already done you a map so I'll leave it with yer and good luck, and Jim, I wouldn't make too many visits to that tomb – go in once, get the gear then get the fuck out of there."

"There's only three of us, we'll never do it in one trip."

"Get some help then, safety in numbers mate, right I'm off, good luck."

It was ten by the time Nick left and I've gone into panic mode not only 'ave I gotta deal with Mike, the coons and the Old Bill, I've now got the curse of Father fucking Morley to deal with. I've alway had a bit of an open mind when it comes to ghosts and spirits, I've never seen one myself but my Mum swears she saw my uncle Sid once. She also used to see this spiritualist woman called Diane and she reckoned spirits were all around us. She said we've all got a spirit guide, and some of the things she told my Mum years ago when I was a kid all seem to 'ave come true, so I suppose if there's good spirits then there's gotta be the odd evil fucker ain't there? I mean it makes sense don't it, you take Hitler for example, he ain't gonna be hovering around 'elping people out is he, nah, course he fucking ain't, he's probably possessed some poor fucker and made 'em do something 'orrible. Well, whether Father Morley is 'anging around that old house or not, like Nick says I've got no choice!

The plans had to be changed: me, Dave and Rudy were still going in the lorry but instead of Ken, Vinny, Ron and Charlie going with the girls on Saturday they were now following us down in the transit we used for delivering bikes. All I told the lads was where the drugs were, I left out the bit about Father Morley and all that spooky shit. Well, we set off nice and early Friday morning, Ken and Vinny followed us down in the transit and we headed off to Shepherds Bush to pick Ron and Charlie up. We left London at eight and we were well on our way. Before we started this little adventure, I made my mind up I weren't gonna get too friendly with Rudy but it's very hard not to like the geezer, he was a good laugh and certainly not your run of the mill dodgy drug dealer, but I remember Ron or Charlie saying he was a bit of a nasty fucker, so I thought I'd ask him what they meant.

"So Rudy, it's been nearly thirty years since I last saw yer, what you been up to?"

"I've done alright Jim, I've got a nice place back home."

"What Brixton?"

"No, Jamaica Jim, my Mum and Dad wanted to end their days back home so I bought 'em a place and when I've sorted this mess out 'm gonna join 'em. I've managed to stay out the nick for nearly thirty years, my luck's gotta run out sooner or later, so I'm gonna quit while I'm ahead."

"Yeah you've been a lucky bastard alright, how you got away with it for so long?"

"You gotta know yer customers Jim, only sell to your regulars and their mates, when did you ever see me go up to anyone and ask if they wanted any gear?"

"Never."

"That's right."

"Yeah, I was unlucky."

"No Jim, you was fuckin' stupid."

"I was desperate mate, that's what I was."

"Yeah you were well fucked up alright."

"When I got out I heard you were a right nasty fucker and you were dead, what was that all about then?"

"It was about sixty-nine I started knocking out LSD, Charlie, and heroin, the hippies were into all that shit. I changed my supplier and started using these wide boys from Essex. The first lot of gear was good shit, so I bought fucking loads of the stuff. Anyway, I knocked it out to my usual clients and this hippie bird overdoses on some bad shit Charlie I sold her and ends up dead. So her mates tried setting me up with the Old Bill but lucky for me, the bird who introduced me to these hippies tipped me off. I've told my supplier I'm lying low for a while and they've gone round to this squat in Finchley and beat the shit out the hippies that are gonna grass me up. I had nothing to do with it, it was all getting a bit too intense so I fucked off back to Jamaica for a few years and waited for it to all calm down, and that's when I got involved with the lot that are on Dave's back and mine now."

"Alright, you didn't do the hippies but it was you that sold that shit to the bird who overdosed?"

"Listen Jim, that shit I sold weren't good and if she'd done a few lines instead of a few grams she would have been alright, is it my faul she was a greedy cow. Let's put it another way, if you go to Tesco and buy four bottles of vodka and drink the fucking lot and kill yourself, it ain't Tesco's fault is it?"

"I suppose not."

"No suppose about it Jim, I don't force 'em to take it, I just supply it, what they decide to do is down to them, I don't really give a shit."

"So you've done alright over the years, you've obviously got a few bob?"

"Like I say Jim, the flights are booked, this time next week I'll be sipping cocktails on a beach in Montego Bay."

Fucking hell, how bad did I feel now. I waited to the next stop and while Rudy went into the service station for a leak I had a word with Dave.

"We gotta do something, we can't let the poor fucker go down."

"Yeah we can, coz if he don't, we will, and do yer think he'd give a shit while he's sitting under a fucking banana tree sipping cocktails, course he fuckin' won't, anyway like he says his been lucky. Alright so he does ten years, he can still retire to the sun. Anyway he's too young to retire, lazy fucker."

"Ain't you got no conscience you heartless fucker?"

"When it comes to Rudy, no I 'aven't, him being so fucking stupid has cost me and Bunny everything, bollocks to him."

Well I could see where Dave's coming from but I weren't too 'appy about it. I can still remember that first night inside lying there in the dark, fucking devastated I was and I didn't 'ave any real future, whereas Rudy has got it all worked out. His flights are booked and everything, how bad is he gonna feel lying in a cell instead of on a beach? But Dave was right, rather him than me.

We got to the island at twelve and booked into the caravan site, me and Dave took the transit to suss out where the old house was, while Rudy and the others had something to eat. The house was about a thirty minute drive from where we were staying. It's a good job we brought the transit coz you would never get the lorry close enough, even in daylight it looked one scary place. We decided the best time to go up there and look for the gear was about one in the morning, so rather than sit round waiting we all went out and had a few beers. It was great, it was like it was 1964 all over again; there were scooters everywhere and the DJ in the boozer was playing a good mix of Motown and Soul with a bit of Who, Small Faces and Yardbirds thrown in for good measure. We rolled out of there at about two, needless to say we were a little bit pissed, it was a fucking good night. The only one who wasn't pissed was Ken, it weren't really his cup of tea, which is a good job really, we needed one of us to 'ave their wits about 'em. We got to the dirt track which led up to the house at about two-thirty and parked the van up against the perimeter fence.

(Jim) "Right lads, this shouldn't take too long, we climb over the fence, head to the back of the house, that's where the graveyard is. We're looking for the biggest one there, it's like a big square stone room with a railing round it, we get the gear and fuck off out of 'ere."

(Vinny) "What do we need sledge hammers for?"

"In case we can't get in the tomb we smash our way in."

Ron and Charlie were the first over the fence, they dropped down over the other side and all we could 'ear was Charlie pissing himself laughing. Ron had landed right in the middle of a blackberry bush and just lay there stuck.

(Ken) "I ain't climbing no fucking fence, stand back."

As we stood back Ken's took a swing with the hammer and started smashing fuck out the fence.

(Jim) "Alright Ken calm down, you'll wake the fuckin' dead."

(Ken) "There's no fucker up 'ere, you said the place is empty."

"Yeah, yeah it is, come on let's go."

We climbed through the hole and started walking up to the house.

(Vinny) "Jim, I thought you said the place was empty, no one had been up 'ere for years."

"Yeah that's right."

"Well who was the geezer on the roof I just see?"

"Bollocks, you're winding me up."

"No straight up, he was standing by the chimney and he was holding something."

"What was he holding?"

"I dunno what it was but he had one in each hand."

"Fucking 'ell, let's get out of 'ere, let's just forget the whole fuckin' thing."

(Dave) "Don't talk so fucking daft, it's probably some old tramp living 'ere."

"That weren't no fucking tramp, that was the ghost of Father Morley."

Ken pissed himself laughing and then the others joined in.

"No fuck off, stop laughing, I'm serious, this place is fucking haunted."

(Ken) Who's this Father Morley then?"

"This place used to be a nut house hundreds of years ago, Father Morley was the priest who used to run it, he was a real evil fucker, he used to torture the patients in the basement. When the villagers found out they killed him but five years later he came back from the dead and he cut a couple of kids' heads off. That's what you saw Vinny, Father Morley holding the kids' heads."

(Dave) "Even if it was a fucking ghost what's he gonna do to seven of us?"

"That ain't the full story, trust me, let's get the fuck out of 'ere."

(Dave) "Right, who wants to go back, oh dear Jim, you're on your own, we'll see you back at the van."

"No, bollocks, I ain't going nowhere on my own, I'm staying with you lot, but don't say I didn't warn yer."

We carried on towards the house. I was shitting myself; as we got closer I kept looking up to the roof but all I could see were them 'orrible stone monsters looking down at me. We walked round the back of the house and in the far corner of the grounds you could just see the outline of the headstones, amongst the brambles and stinging nettles.

"There it is lads, over there."

(Ron) "It's like a fucking jungle."

(Charlie) "It's a bit like being in a horror film ain't it."

(Jim) "Yer and what always 'appens, I tell yer what 'appens, one by one they all get bumped off and that's what's gonna 'appen to us."

(Charlie) "Fuck off Jim, you're scaring me now."

(Ron) "Yeah, now I'm starting to sober up I think I'll head back to the van with you Jim."

(Dave) "No one's going anywhere until we've got that gear, now let's split up and start looking for that tomb."

(Ron) "Fuck off Dave, let's stick together, it ain't gonna take that long."

(Ken) "Yeah let's stick together."

(Vinny) "What's up, scared are yer, I thought you was a bit tasty."

Vinny thought it'd be funny winding Ken up by making chicken noises.

(Ken) "I'll show yer how fucking tasty I am, if you don't shut the fuck up."

(Rudy) "Hey lads, chill out."

(Ken) "Bollocks."

(Rudy) "Come on lads, it ain't that bad."

(Ken) "Na, I don't suppose it is for you."

(Rudy) "What do yer mean by that?"

(Ken) "All these fucking trees and bushes, I bet you feel at home, you being a fucking jungle bunny and all that."

(Rudy) "Fuck you."

(Ken) "Do yer wanna try, do yer?"

(Jim) "Come on lads leave it out, look, over there, that's gotta be it."

Over by this big old tree was the tomb; it must have been about thirty or forty foot square. We couldn't open the oak doors so Ken smashed 'em with the sledge hammer. Inside were five stone coffins, one in each corner and one in the middle; we was all shitting ourselves now, even Ken, and I didn't think anything scared him.

(Dave) "There's nothing 'ere."

(Jim) "Nick said there was some sort of secret tunnel linking the tomb to the house."

Charlie was shining his torch all round the walls and tapping 'em with the hammer.

(Vinny) "Charlie, what the fuck you doing?"

"I'm looking for a lever or some sort of secret door."

(Dave) "It's a square stone room you prat."

"Yeah I know but on the films that's what always 'appens ain't it, someone leans on a candle holder or coat hanger then the door opens."

(Ken) "You've been watching too much Scooby Doo, you silly fucker, if there's any link between 'ere and the house it's gotta be a tunnel."

Ken started walking round tapping the floor with the hammer. He hit an area near the middle and it was wood, we scraped the dust and dirt away and there were two doors and in the middle was a big stone angel holding 'em shut.

(Jim) "That's why Nick's mate Steve was never seen again, someone or something trapped him down there."

(Charlie) "Hang on a minute, who's this Steve?"

"Well when the gear was brought up from the beach Steve was taking it off and hiding it; when the Old Bill steamed in they didn't get Steve but Nick reckons he was never seen again."

(Ron) "I ain't fuckin' going down there."

(Charlie) "No, screw that."

(Rudy) "Yeah, we could all end up trapped."

Ken started smashing the angel up.

(Ken) "Problem solved, no one's putting that back are they? Now let's open it up, get the gear and get out of 'ere."

(Charlie) "What if someone puts one of them stone coffins on it?"

(Ken) "Don't be fucking stupid, they ain't going nowhere, they must weight a ton."

(Ron) "Yeah, so did that angel but somehow it ended up on them doors."

Ken then started to smash the doors to pieces.

(Ken) 'appy now, there ain't any doors."

(Dave) "Look, that shit can't be far down there if he was doing it on his own. I'll stay 'ere with Ken and you lot get down there and start looking."

(Charlie) "Why do you get to stay up 'ere?"

"Alright, you stay up 'ere and I'll go down, come on let's get this done, it'll be daylight soon."

Dave climbed down the tunnel followed by Rudy, then Vinny, then me and Ron on the end. I made sure I weren't last coz in the horror films it's always the one in the front or the back that cops it first. The tunnel was ice cold. We'd walked up it about a hundred foot when we came to the first room; we shone the torches in and there it was, twelve cases. We grabbed one each and headed back. We got 'em back into the tomb then went back for the rest. As we made our way back Dave stopped.

(Dave) "Did you 'ear that?"

(Rudy) "Hear what?"

"It was like a moaning noise."

(Ron) "Yeah I heard it."

(Vinny) "No but I heard it that time."

I heard it as well, it was like a groaning noise coming from further up the tunnel. We were about ten foot from the room so we quickly grabbed a case each and the noise was getting louder. Not only was it getting louder but the whole room got colder and there was a really bad smell like rotten eggs. At first I thought Ron had shit himself but that smell couldn't have come from any human, not even Ken smelt like that after a night on the piss followed by a couple of kebabs! We got out the room and into the tunnel. Dave shone his torch up the tunnel and there was like a mist, and in the mist there were faces. Well that was it, we legged it. I 'ave never run so fast in my life, Ron and Rudy were screaming like a couple of kids on a ghost train. We got to the steps leading out the tunnel and it was a fucking free for all, it was every man for themselves. Ken and Charlie helped us out, we grabbed a couple of bags each and we were out that tomb in seconds, we were fucked. I thought I was gonna 'ave a fucking heart attack. I couldn't get my breath but then Charlie looked back and the mist was coming out the tomb. That was it, we were off again, sprinting down the hill for dear life. Ken was out front and we were heading for the fence, he was running so fast he couldn't stop. He got to within a few feet of the fence and fell arse over tit and went straight through it. It was seconds before we all followed, we got in the van and we were out of there. We drove about four miles down the road and pulled into a car park by the beach. We all got out and just collapsed on the beach. We all just lay there for about five minutes and no one said anything, we were all in shock.

"I told yer didn't I, I fucking warned yer, but you weren't 'aving none of it was yer?"

(Dave) "Yeah well we got away with it, we got the gear."

"Let's hope we did get away with it."

(Ken) "What do yer mean let's hope, we 'ave?"

(Charlie) "Is there something you not telling us Jim?"

"If you'd all bothered to listen to me I would of told yer the full story."

(Ron) "Go on then, we're listening."

"Well, after the First World War this Yank bought the house and lived there with his wife and two kids; he ended up killing 'em all, then himself."

(Charlie) "Fuckin' 'ell."

"Well the thing is, everyone reckoned he was possessed by Father Morley."

(Dave) "Why's that then?"

"Well he cut his kids' heads off."

(Rudy) "Shit, man."

(Dave) "Well none of us were up there long enough."

(Ken) "I don't know, Vinny's a bit quiet, he ain't jumped inside yer has he?"

As soon as Ken said it Vinny screamed, grabbed Ron in a headlock and spun him round, everyone pissed themselves laughing and we headed off back to the caravan site where we transferred the gear onto the lorry. Saturday morning me, Ken and Dave loaded the scooters up and got everything ready for Monday morning, then we all headed off into town for something to eat. It's funny coz none of us mentioned what 'appened that night, I think we were all still in shock. I mean you see that sort of thing on films and you hear ghost stories, like my Mum saw my uncle Sid, and you always doubt it but there was seven of us and trust me they were there alright, we all saw 'em, make no mistake!

By the time the girls got there at three, the island was buzzing with the sound of scooters everywhere, there were thousands. The only one who weren't loving it was Ken, he thought grown men bombing round on scooters was a bit silly. Well I didn't give a shit about Ken, this might have been my last two nights of freedom for a very long time, so I was gonna enjoy it. We all ended up in a lively boozer in town that was having a karaoke night, we all had a go but the star of the night was Rudy, he done a cracking version of Jackie Wilson's Your Love Keeps Lifting Me (Higher and Higher). Rudy was a great laugh, even Ken was starting to like him and Ken don't like anyone who ain't one hundred percent English.

Needless to say we all woke up Sunday morning with raging hangovers. All we had planned for the day was a nice relaxing day on the beach, that was until Vinny started looking round a scooter, then hit us with the bombshell, "I'm looking forward to 'aving a go on one of these, they look a lot of fun."

(Ken) "A lot of fun, they're fucking horrible."

(Jim) "Please tell me you've been on one before?"

"No I ain't, they look easy enough, poxy things only do about thirty don't they?"

(Ken) "About fifty, sixty if the wind's behind yer but you don't wanna be doing that coz the brakes are shit and in the wet they're fucking lethal."

(Dave) "You didn't think to tell us this last week?"

"What's the big deal, I'll soon get the hang of it."

(Jim) "The big deal is you're gonna be getting the hang of it with a few million quid's worth of gear on it."

(Charlie) "Well get one off the lorry and let him ride round on it, by the end of the day he'll be alright."

"I didn't want them scooters off the lorry 'til Monday when we're ready to go, you don't know if we're being watched. If the drug squad are watching us they'll clock the reg then Monday when that ferry docks, they'll 'ave all of us."

(Dave) "They ain't interested in us, it's Mike's lot they're after."

"Yeah well, I ain't taking any chances."

(Ken) "Right, 'ere's what we do, back the transit up close to the lorry, we quickly throw one of the scooters on then take it out to that old air strip we passed and let Vinny 'ave a practice, no one's gonna see us."

Well we didn't 'ave no choice, Vinny had to 'ave a practice, there was no way he was gonna jump on a scooter for the first time and ride it out the back of a lorry. It's a good job we let him have a practice, instead of letting the clutch out slowly he just let go of it, the scooter's shot off without him and gone skidding on its side. It took him a couple of hours but he soon got the 'ang of it. We loaded it back on the lorry, a little bit bruised and battered but it was still OK to ride, then we headed off to town to grab something to eat.

Me, Dave and Vinny decided to go over everything one last time then meet the others later.

"Right, we're all set, tomorrow's the big day, I think we've got everything covered."

(Vinny) "I don't get why we've gotta fuck around with the lorry, there's gotta be at least forty scooters leaving this site tomorrow, why don't we just unload 'em tonight and ride off with everyone tomorrow?"

(Dave) "Yeah he's got a point Jim, I don't think the Old Bill 'ave been watching us, all the attention will be at the ferry terminal at Portsmouth, they're waiting for six blokes on scooters and a bloody great lorry. Why don't we load Rudy's gear on the transit, let him take that instead and at least it gives the poor fucker a sporting chance?"

"I agree about leaving the site with all the others but what about Charles the copper, I've told him Rudy's in the lorry, he ain't gonna be too 'appy I'm not straight with him."

(Dave) "Get Ken to fuck the lorry up in some way and tell him it broke down."

(Vinny) "It doesn't matter if Rudy's in the lorry or van, the meet with the coons is still the same, they'll still get 'em."

"Yeah alright, we'll get Ken to sort it later."

(Vinny) "The other thing is, I don't trust my old man and I certainly don't trust the Old Bill."

(Jim) "Nor do I, but we ain't got no choice 'ave we?"

"Course we 'ave, the ball's well and truly in our court, once that ferry docks we've got all day Monday to put that shit wherever we want, why put it where my old man wants it?"

"Coz if we put it anywhere else don't you think your old man is gonna be a little bit suspicious when the Old Bill nick 'em all?"

"Yeah course he will, but we'll put it down to that bent copper Dickson, I'll tell my old man he tipped us off, that the Lewisham drop was hot and he told us to change the drop to the club."

(Dave) "He's got a point Jim, that unit in Lewisham has probably got the Old Bill round it even now."

"If we drop the gear at the club we're gonna be safe as houses mate, all the Old Bill are interested in is Mike and the coons and we're still giving 'em what they want. It don't matter whatever way you look at it there's a risk, but I agree with Vinny at least if we drop it at the club there's less chance we're gonna get nicked but a slight chance you might and it don't matter where we drop it, you're taking that chance."

"Alright we'll drop it at the club Monday afternoon, I'll ring Mike and the copper Monday night and tell 'em the change of drop."

Well, Sunday night we just had a quiet drink, it's bad enough riding a scooter over a hundred miles but to do it with a hangover would have been a nightmare. Monday morning we got up nice and early, loaded the scooters up and we were ready to go; we said our goodbyes to Rudy and the girls and we left along with at least thirty others. It was about a twenty minute ride to the ferry terminal and at practically every road junction we were joined by more scooters, by the time we got to the terminal there must have been over a hundred scooters.

The crossing was about half an hour so we just had time for a quick cup of tea. The ferry docked at about eleven-thirty and if there was any Old Bill waiting there, all they would have seen as the ferry opened up was a thick cloud of two stroke smoke, and even if we had dirty great name tags on our parkas they would still have had trouble picking us out. There were scooters everywhere all shooting off in different directions. The plan was to stick with as many scooters as possible and never let there just be the six of us. Ken stayed at the back and if anyone broke down only Ken would stop, but thankfully we all made it to Kew Bridge. Once we crossed the Thames, we were well on our way, we didn't have to worry coz the Old Bill were expecting six scooters to be heading round the South Circular Road and not the north.

We got to the club at about six and unloaded the gear, we made it. As soon as we got back on them scooters and headed off back to Dave's and the bike shop, we were in the clear. The drugs were sitting in the club and there was nothing to link us to 'em, all I needed to do now was ring Charles and let him know so he had plenty of time to get his blokes there, then once I got the nod from him I just had to tell Mike. We all stayed at Dave's that night and got well pissed, we had a lot to celebrate: me and Dave were in the clear, Ron and Charlie were gonna end up with fifty grand and Ken could pay off the taxman so his job was safe, and Vinny would be rid of his old man and hopefully 'ave the club. Well, on the Tuesday everything went to plan. Mike himself turned up at the club with five of his best blokes. There were a few shots fired but the only casualty was Mike; he keeled over and had a heart attack, they reckon he was dead before he hit the ground. Dickson the bent copper got nicked along with his dodgy son, and as for poor old Rudy and the Jamaicans, Charles reckoned there was no one nicked, as expected they went out in a blaze of glory. I felt bad about Rudy but like Dave said, rather him than us. All we needed to do now is get the gear that Ken had hid in the spare tyres and sell it to Dave's contact. Dave headed off to Kent late Saturday afternoon; the plan was for all of us to 'ave a proper celebration at the Punch Bowl Saturday night then split the cash Sunday morning. Everything went like clockwork, Dave got the cash and stashed it in the safe at the bike shop. We all met at the White Lion for a few drinks then headed off to the Punch Bowl to meet Vinny in his new club. We got to the club at about nine, but instead of Vinny waiting to meet us at the door Roger was there instead.

"Took your time didn't yer, we was expecting you lot about an hour ago. Go straight upstairs, Vinny's got yer a couple of tables and the drinks in. Jim, lets go to the office, I just want a quick word before you get too pissed."

It felt good walking through the Punch Bowl again, it was packed and there was a great band playing.

"Come in Jim, sit down, Vinny's been filling me in about your little adventure, you've had quite an eventful weekend."

"Yeah you could say that, it was a bit of a laugh as it goes."

"Yeah it sounds it. Right, I'll get straight to the point, I know you're dying to get out there. The Punch Bowl, Jim, Vinny's old man promised it to him."

"That's right."

"Well it weren't never gonna 'appen."

"Yeah, I didn't think Mike would keep to his word."

"It weren't gonna 'appen Jim coz it wasn't Mike's to give away, it's mine."

"Yours?"

"That's right, the deeds, everything, it's all in my name. Yeah, while Mike was around it was all part of the firm but now he's gone the whole fucking lot's been split. Tony has copped the villa in Spain, Alex the accountant, he's 'appy he's got the shares from four of Mike's businesses and Phil, Dave and Rob are running the fruit machines and protection."

"What 'appened to Ray?"

"He's running a club down in Southend."

"You say the Punch Bowl weren't Mike's to give away, well it ain't all yours is it, half of it was mine till you fucking robbed it off me."

"You were a silly fucker Jim, you know what your trouble is don't yer?"

"What's that then?"

"You trust too easy, you was quite 'appy leaving everything to me while you were playing the big I am club owner, you're no fucking businessman Jim, but I tell yer what you are."

"A fucking idiot."

"No Jim, you're a good bloke, I like yer Jim, you make me laugh

189

and when you were running this with me we worked well didn't we?"

"Yeah."

"The thing is Jim, I ain't a greedy fucker and that's why I'm giving you your half back."

"You serious?"

"I'm serious alright, but there's one problem, what we gonna do about Vinny? I mean that poor fucker's left without nothing and he's out there thinking he owns the fucking lot."

"Fuck it, he can 'ave half of my share."

"I can read you like a book Jim, Alex has already got the paperwork drafted and ready to sign, it's a three way split, what do yer reckon?"

"I reckon I need to shake your hand and get seriously pissed, but before I do, what was Dickson on about, he reckoned that he had a statement from you putting me in the frame for the fire, and what if Mike didn't croak it?"

"Dickson had fuck all on yer, that's why he planted that gear at your place and whether Mike croaked it or not he was always gonna go down for handling that shit, and with a dodgy ticker like his, he was only ever gonna get out of the nick in a wooden box. Now you get out there with your mates and 'ave that drink, you deserve it Jim."

I had that drink alright, I walked out that office and I was buzzing, I just stood at the top of the balcony, looked down at the dance floor and the band and just soaked up the atmosphere. After five long years I finally got my club back, now I really had something to celebrate. I grabbed four bottles of champagne from behind the bar and got back to the others just as Dave started telling the girls about the old house and Father Morley. I don't think they believed us and to be honest, if I hadn't seen it for myself I don't think I would have either, but we had a right laugh telling 'em.

It was turning into a great night, we all had something to celebrate. I didn't think the night could get any better but at about half ten the band started playing Your Love Keeps Lifting Me…, we looked down and there was Rudy on stage giving it large, we couldn't believe it, we all thought he was fucking dead. It turns out that Dave used his old house in Kent for the drop with the Jamaicans coz he had the perfect escape route planned for Rudy all along. Well, needless to say we were all well chuffed, Rudy being alive was the icing on the cake, even Ken was pleased. It was one of those nights you didn't want to end and it didn't; when the club shut at two we all stayed on well into Sunday morning 'aving a laugh about the past and deciding where we go from 'ere.

Well, Rudy stuck to his plans and flew off to Jamaica; he'd had nearly thirty years of dealing and never got done but this little episode scared the shit out of him so he decided to quit while he's ahead. I gave Ken a second chance at running the shop, only on the condition that Sarah done the books and looked after the cash and Ken got some help with his gambling addiction. He reckoned he didn't 'ave a problem but anyone who sticks fifty grand on a fucking horse has got one serious problem in my book. Dave and Bunny stayed on at the flat and managed to talk Judy, Ron and Charlie into investing their money into the sex industry. Dave reckoned he was onto something big with his visiting massage service, he even had Vinny driving girls around on his nights off.

Me, I hate to admit it, after years of dealing with gangsters, bent coppers, psychos and even fucking ghosts, I wanted a bit of normality with Tracy. If I had my time again I wouldn't change a thing, even the eight years inside. My old man always said I was nuts, a bleedin' schizophrenic that's what you are, split personality, he said, and in a way I suppose he was right. I never knew who I was, I always wanted to be a somebody but you know what, after all the shit I've been through I'm a happy man and I now know who I am. I'm Jimmy, who the fuck are you?

I hope you enjoyed *To Be Someone*.
www.tobesomeone.co.uk
if you would like to add your comments.